A Menopausal
Gentleman

TRIANGULATIONS
Lesbian/Gay/Queer ▲ Theater/Drama/Performance

Series Editors
Jill Dolan, Princeton University
David Román, University of Southern California

A Menopausal Gentleman

THE SOLO PERFORMANCES OF PEGGY SHAW

Peggy Shaw

EDITED AND WITH AN
INTRODUCTION BY

JILL DOLAN

The University of Michigan Press | Ann Arbor

Published in the United States of America by
The University of Michigan Press
Printed and bound by CPI Group (UK) Ltd, Croydon, CR0 4YY

2014 2013 2012 2011   4 3 2 1

A CIP catalog record for this book is available from the British Library.

Library of Congress Cataloging-in-Publication Data

Shaw, Peggy.
    A menopausal gentleman : the solo performances of Peggy Shaw /
edited and with an introduction by Jill Dolan.
        p. cm. — (Triangulations: lesbian, gay, and queer theater)
    Includes bibliographical references.
    ISBN 978-0-472-11647-8 (cloth : alk. paper) —
    ISBN 978-0-472-03414-7 (pbk. : alk. paper)
        1. Lesbians—Drama. 2. Lesbians' writings, American. 3. American
drama—20th century. 4. Shaw, Peggy. 5. Women performance
artists—United States—Biography. I. Dolan, Jill, 1957– II. Title.
    PS3569.H38428M46   2011
    792.7092—dc22   2011011889

Photo credits: photo on page 43 from *You're Just Like My Father,* by Eva Weiss;
photo on page 67 from *Menopausal Gentleman,* by Craig Bailey; photos on pages 99
and 129 from *To My Chagrin,* by Dona Ann McAdams; and photo on page 133 from
Must, by Manual Vason @MVS STudio, 2009.

I dedicate this book to Lois Weaver

who, among many other things, in real life and in Split Britches,
taught me how to transform myself
from the brutal political smoking aggressive street criminal
lesbian mother butch obvious
cabaret performer I was when she met me 33 years ago
to the more subtle mature loving illogical polished anarchist
lesbian grandmother that
I am today.

And to all directors and collaborators everywhere
who make "solo" shows possible.

—PEGGY SHAW

CONTENTS

CONTENTS

Introduction: A Certain Kind of Successful

JILL DOLAN

This is how I was born. I was born like this . . . this is how I walk. I never make it up. I didn't construct this person for your pleasure. I'm performing as myself. Part of how I take care of people is that they don't have to be anything else except how they are. And I've been surviving as an artist for thirty years.

—PEGGY SHAW

Obie-award-winning performer/writer Peggy Shaw has plied her self-fashioned gender-bending performances in off Broadway, re-gional, and international performance venues for the last forty years. As a self-described butch lesbian, Shaw's on- and offstage performances of masculinity have brought her a certain renown and a committed fan following. Those who have seen the solo per-formances collected in this anthology of her work—*You're Just Like My Father* (1993), *Menopausal Gentleman* (1997), *To My Chagrin* (2001), and *Must—The Inside Story* (2008), which she's toured around the country and internationally since the early 1990s—at-test to the vitality and seductiveness of her stage presence. Those who know her as a friend, teacher, or colleague testify to Shaw's singular attention to their development as artists or activists dedi-cated to changing the world. Shaw cuts an imposing figure, whether striding through Manhattan's East Village, where she's lived most of her adult life, or speaking on panels about theater and performance, sexuality and gender, cutting through the niceties by stating her ideas baldly and vividly. Shaw's potent spirit infuses her work and her entire existence; her resilience and her talent, her insights and her fortitude make her an iconic figure in lesbian, queer, and feminist performance.

For the first half of her career, Shaw was part of the Split Britches performance trio with Lois Weaver and Deb Margolin, which, shortly after its establishment in 1980, became the most renowned feminist theater troupe in the world. Split Britches' galvanizing mix of personal narrative and feminist, ethnic, and class-based history, its easy transitions from poignant memory pieces to the idioms of American vaudeville and its funny shtick, and its three performers' virtuosic claims on a performance style they virtually invented moved what had been earnest, didactic theater for women into a whole new realm. As theater historian Charlotte Canning has documented, feminist performance in the 1970s grew from the consciousness-raising meetings that catalyzed the political movement and often used agitprop to depict the newly understood experiences of women. Groups such as It's All Right to Be Woman Theatre shared felt truths about women's experience by engaging audiences in direct testimony, using Brechtian techniques as well as homegrown devices like "crankies," rolls of paper depicting political aphorisms that were wound out across makeshift stages. Likewise, the Women's Experimental Theatre, in the mid- to late 1970s and early 1980s, relied on witnessing techniques to structure relationships between performers and audiences. Roberta Sklar, Sondra Segal, and Clare Coss adapted classic Greek texts to inform their feminist reorientations in *The Daughters' Cycle Trilogy* (1977–80), for example, which gathered stories told in workshops from numerous women's lives to inform its political urgency. This feminist theater work was incisive, topical, and activist, full of advocacy for women's potential. It demonstrated deep investments in revising theater with the content of women's lives and experiences and stretched the possibilities of what the form could offer to women.

In this context, Split Britches' performances demonstrated that feminist theater could also avail itself of popular forms and humor and still offer a valid social critique. With their intricate, poetic use of metaphor; their play with gender roles and ethnicity; their use of personal memory, as well as a range of popular cultural texts; their experiments with nonlinear, imagistic, and sometimes highly ironic storytelling; and their often bawdy, ribald humor, they provided an alternative feminist theater. Their scripts were inspired by their own dreams and desires, which the trio's creative alchemy transformed into condensed nuggets of keenly drawn moments of pure theater. Collaborating with Lois Weaver, who for many years was Shaw's life partner as well as her most frequent leading lady, and Deb Margolin, whose poetic, Jewish, heterosexual, sometimes macabre imagination served as the primary shaper of the trio's texts, Shaw anchored Split Britches with her tall, imposing, butch lesbian presence. (Shaw shares many anecdotes in which people describe her as "tall" when what they really mean is "masculine.") Her working-class Belmont, Massachusetts, accent always echoed musically beside Weaver's southern lilt and Margolin's northeastern Jewish inflections; Shaw's open-vowel style played the bass to their violin and viola. Shaw's work with Weaver and Margolin secured the threesome's notorious gender play. Standing nearly six feet tall, Shaw towered over the other two with her ramrod, muscular power. Whether she wore the thin cotton dress and bandana of the sister Della in the troupe's signature piece, *Split Britches* (1981), the shiny cheap chiffon gown of the lesbian mother performing a scene from *Shanghai Gesture* in *Upwardly Mobile Home* (1984), or the bustier, garter belt, and hose of the queer sister trapped in a world of rental clothes and fantasy in *Dress Suits to Hire* (1987)—the two-hander Shaw performed with Weaver and wrote with performance artist Holly Hughes—Shaw has always been a stunning presence in the feminist and lesbian performance world. Weaver says, "I've always loved . . . her brashness, her bigness, her loudness. You know, as much as it drives me crazy, I love it. . . .

Someone used to say, 'Lois whispers and Peggy shouts.' . . . [S]he embodied things I thought."[1]

In *Split Britches,* Weaver, with her ironized, self-consciously exaggerated femininity, served as the femme front person onstage, reaching out directly to spectators to frame the play's tales and contextualize the characters, who were drawn from her own family in the Blue Ridge Mountains of Virginia. Margolin's more eccentrically feminine, palpable intellectualism was layered with her impersonation of an elderly, nearly mad sister who made peculiar noises and fantasized throughout the play. Standing upstage of Weaver and Margolin, Shaw—whose work Weaver calls "incredibly disciplined"—brought a stolid, fierce charisma to the play. In the "pictures" for which the trio posed in *Split Britches* by projecting the empty light of a slide projector over their live, still tableaux, Shaw's Della was a harbinger of everything Shaw would bring to fifteen years' worth of Split Britches' performances and later her own solo work: handsome intelligence; unmediated physicality, regardless of her masculine or feminine garb; a risky, raw style that made her galvanizing to watch; just a hint of violence in her resistance to a dominant culture that damned and demeaned everything she and her characters represented; and a fierce dedication to women, whether the two onstage with her, those in the immediate audience, or the fictional ones she created from a glimmer of her own experience and dreams.

Split Britches also began an investigation into the way socioeconomic class shapes women's lives, a focus that Shaw would carry into her solo work. The characters in *Split Britches* lived on very little, but their resourcefulness was palpably evident onstage in ways that pointed to how women's material lives shape them as subjects. The women in *Split Britches* made biscuits throughout the play, rolling out the dough, kneading it, tamping it down with the heels of their hands, using the liveness of theater to enact and ennoble

---

1. Unless otherwise noted, all quotations from Shaw are from her interview with Jill Dolan and Jaclyn Pryor in Austin, Texas, 18 April 2005. Unless otherwise noted, all quotations from Weaver are from her interview with Jill Dolan and Jaclyn Pryor in Austin, Texas, 23 April 2005.

women's work. In *Upwardly Mobile Home,* too, Shaw, Weaver, and Margolin demonstrated the ingenuity of women trying to scrape out a living by harnessing an entrepreneurial, seat-of-their-pants spirit of determination not often required by people more securely ensconced in the middle class. In the salient gesture of her first solo show, *You're Just Like My Father,* Shaw wraps elastic bandages around her chest and fists, the way a boxer wraps her hands when preparing for a fight. But that action, too, makes plain how intimately one's body is engaged in work. Shaw evokes the labor of fighting, performing, and living in richly material ways.

Split Britches collaborated for nearly two decades, with each new production demonstrating how women could harness the power of theater to provide a social and aesthetic forum. After working together as a group, Shaw, Weaver, and Margolin began in the mid-1990s to work in other configurations, creating solo performances, seeking out partnerships with other artists, or, in Shaw and Weaver's case, collaborating together on duets that stretched the bounds of the antic, poignant form they had created with Margolin. *Anniversary Waltz* (1989) was Weaver and Shaw's first performance alone together; eventually, they used their common stage time to chart the real-life pressures and pleasures of growing into and out of a long-term personal and professional relationship. *Lesbians Who Kill* (1993), written in collaboration with Margolin, is a noir tale in which Shaw and Weaver huddle in a car together through a storm, outside a house they're afraid will be struck by lightning. Loosely based on the life of lesbian Aileen Wuornos, a serial killer who was eventually executed by lethal injection in Florida in 2002, the piece is replete with the potential for violence enacted both by and toward the two women. *Lust and Comfort* (1994–95), on which they collaborated with London's Gay Sweatshop, addressed the constraints and complacencies of staying in a relationship and "the urge to reinvent desire." *It's a Small House and We Lived in It Always* (2001), a collaboration between Split Britches and Clod Ensemble, is a melancholy, darkly funny piece that also rehearses the themes of intimacy as both entrapment and safety.

Shaw's solo work remains happily entrenched in the nonlinear, imagistic, melancholic yet hopeful, dark but funny style that Split Britches pioneered. The performance scripts collected in *A Menopausal Gentleman* follow the trajectory of manhood as Shaw has performed and lived it as a butch lesbian. In *You're Just Like My Father,* Shaw explores how she learned to "be a man." In *Menopausal Gentleman,* she suffers the hormonal storms of her changing female body while maintaining her chivalrous, handsome, compelling masculine exterior. In *To My Chagrin,* dedicated to her biracial grandson, Ian, who was born in 1994, she debates how to pass on her refashioned and revised masculinity to a child whose own life is shaped by the many facets of race as much as Shaw's is by the multiplicities of gender.

Shaw's work has garnered national and international recognition. She has received three Obie awards—the accolade bestowed by the *Village Voice* to off and off-off Broadway theater—the first for her stellar turn in the original 1987 production of *Dress Suits to Hire,* which was revived in April 2005 in Austin, Texas, then moved for a well-received three-week run at LaMama in New York City. She garnered her two additional Obies for her work with Split Britches. Shaw received New York Foundation for the Arts Emerging Forms awards in 1988, 1995, and 1999 and in 1995 received an Anderson Foundation Stonewall award for excellence in "making the world a better place for gays and lesbians." She has toured internationally, performing with other artists and in her solo shows. Her artistry has been recognized repeatedly with reviews in the *New York Times, Village Voice, Boston Globe, Manchester Guardian, Time Out,* and other major publications. Shaw's appeal has never been confined to lesbian subcultures but has always captivated audiences mixed across sexualities and genders, as well as races, ethnicities, and classes.

The Itinerant Performer: Traveling with Drag Queens

When Peggy Shaw ambles into a room in men's khaki working pants and ankle-high brown boots, her snowy white tank T-shirt worn loosely under a softly printed habanera shirt, jingling the thick chain hooked to her belt, which curves into her back pants pocket to secure her wallet, it's difficult to resist her energy. Shaw's gaze is direct and acute. Under eyebrows that never seem to stop moving as she shapes her strongly held opinions, she peers out at people, cutting away the formalities to get down to the business of truth. A conversation with Shaw runs the gamut from the most personal to the most public issues, which Shaw engages with keen, incisive political critique as well as heartfelt emotion. Shaw doesn't chat. Her intensity requires long, intimate conversations, whether she's talking to one person over cheese and crackers after a performance or speaking to seventy-five people in a question-and-answer session in a university classroom. She's the kind of person who makes a room feel small with her largeness of spirit and her easy ability to bring herself close to people. When Shaw looks out from over her rectangular tortoiseshell glasses while her eyebrows arch, gazing down the length of her Romanesque nose nestled in the middle of the crinkly skin of her Irish face, and runs her fingers through hair cropped short but full, the openness of her expression demands to be reciprocated.

Shaw's generation of Americans came of age in the 1960s and 1970s convinced they could unshackle themselves from convention. But before she came out, Shaw married, when she was very young, since such a choice was then expected of women. She soon left her husband, a white man of German descent, and with her toddler daughter, Shara, in tow, Shaw moved from Massachusetts to New York City. Shaw tells the story of her entrée into performance as a single stroke of fate. She and her young daughter wandered into Sheridan Square in the West Village of Manhattan one day in the late 1960s and stumbled on the glamour drag group Hot Peaches, which was performing in the triangular park where West 4th Street, Christopher Street, and Seventh Avenue collide in a jumble. Shaw relates that she was captivated by these men's performances and decided to hook her star to theirs. She began working with Hot Peaches in a support capacity as a scenic artist since drag queens could only conceive of lesbians as crew members at the time. But Shaw says that outsiders always saw her as a drag queen like the others—her statuesque, masculine form aligned well with the men's, and she became, to outsiders and insiders alike, one of the boy/girls.

Around 1975, Hot Peaches spontaneously decided to do a "gay tour" of Europe for which they had no prior bookings and the phone number for only one contact. As she tells Craig Lucas in an interview in *Bomb,* Shaw, undaunted, loaded a backpack with a few pieces of clothing for herself and her young daughter and off they went on tour. A short time into the trip, when the troupe was squatting in London, Hot Peaches' director Jimmy Camicia got them their first booking at the Oval Theatre, a notably gay friendly venue in South London. Camicia told Shaw, "We're doing a show and we need lesbian material and for you to be in it, so go write something." Shaw says:

> Jimmy just said, "Go in my room over there in the Oval Theatre and come out in fifteen minutes and show me what you write. That's going to be your monologue." So I did, and that was the first thing I ever wrote. I performed it the next week. For the first time in my life. [I]t was called "Dyke." I just started screaming "dyke," "faggot," and all the things people scream at me. . . . It's all about the street. . . . The show we were doing was the *Divas of Sheridan Square.* Jimmy . . . just put me and Shara into it. And I did my "Dyke" monologue, and we just sat and made our costumes from the garbage with everybody else.

If invention comes from necessity, the genesis of Shaw's career as a performer began with a kind of trashy brilliance that only drag queens could inspire.

Shaw doesn't knock her training. On the contrary, she's proud of how she learned on the street, how her performance talents were honed hand in hand with the survival skills necessary for making it through the 1960s and 1970s as an itinerant performer and a single mother touring with a small child. She says, "I can still only write that way. And that's how I teach writing." In fact, Shaw now thrills to being a teacher because the students with whom she works at universities, colleges, and community-based locations around the world are "all going to make the future. . . . And it's my job to reach them in some way and say, 'Hey, this isn't like all it can be, really.' . . . And the white students and the rich ones, I tell them, 'Get out of school. . . . [G]et out of this fucking school and go start a theater. . . . With forty thousand dollars a year you can . . . build a building or something. Or make a play. Don't give it to this college.'"

Shaw makes an example of her own urgency to speak, to come up with something to say on the spot, which lets her tap a deep well of emotional and political resources drawn from her own experiences and the trenchant cultural analysis that fuels the power of her teaching and performances. For example, she tells stories of being harassed on the New York subways in the early 1970s by gangs of hostile young boys and fighting back. She and her friends had rules of engagement: "The first rule is ignore them. Second rule is move. And the third was punch your way out." When forced into the third option, Shaw let her anger fly, putting her fists into action and scaring the boys enough to send them running out of her subway car. Enacting that violent retribution also gave her a taste of overt social performance; her actions were much appreciated by her fellow subway riders. "[E]veryone applauded," Shaw recalls. She remembers this as a time when "women and queers and people of color" all decided "we're not going to take this anymore. It was a beautiful time. It was a scary time."

On the Hot Peaches tour, Shaw and the drag queens crossed paths with Spiderwoman Theatre, a feminist, mostly Native American women's theater company traveling the same ad hoc international circuit. Shaw soon left Hot Peaches to perform with the women, and there she met Weaver, who was part of the Spiderwoman troupe. They became lovers and eventually began developing a performance and political project at odds with Spiderwoman's gestalt. Weaver notes that as she and Shaw performed with Spiderwoman, "even before we became lovers, we immediately established this kind of erotic backstory. Of course you know that wasn't even part of the explicit narrative. I think we really connected on that level of power. How can we between us create that sort of tension that says lesbian?" In 1980, they spun off their own company, forming Split Britches with Margolin.[2]

Originally, Shaw relates, another woman was going to write their eponymous *Split Britches* play with Shaw and Weaver. But Shaw says before the script was finished, two weeks before they were scheduled to open, the woman "blew town and we never saw her again. So we had to start talking as the characters. That's how we learned how to do it. We started talking as the characters and we made the show." But eventually Shaw and Weaver missed the presence of "somebody who could really write." They had heard that Deb Margolin "was like a poet and stuff, so we asked her to write a couple of monologues. And we really liked them. We asked her to be in the show to play Lois's great-aunt and she loved it. And that's how we started working together. . . . And she was funny. She was really funny. Then it was like fourteen years we were together."

Shaw grew up working-class Irish in Belmont, a suburb of Boston, and has been an itinerant artist her entire life.[3] The kind of work she has produced and the venues in which she has worked have precluded a leisured, or even a middle-class, life. Creating performance from scratch as Split Britches did, later devising the solo pieces collected here based on invitations from colleges and universities, touring down-at-the-heel performance spaces—all of this has required Shaw to husband her resources and curb her expectations about creature comforts. As a result, Shaw is one of the few

2. Shaw admits to some tension between her and Weaver and the founders of the Spiderwoman troupe over both aesthetic styles and sexual identity. Although the "bad blood" has since been cleared, the friction seemed to stem from the lesbian baiting that happened throughout the feminist movement at the time, as well as from differences of opinion about appropriate styles of performing.

3. Lesbian feminist scholar Sue-Ellen Case, who edited the 1996 Lambda-award-winning collection of Split Britches' plays, *Split Britches: Lesbian Practice/Feminist Performance,* has in fact called Shaw a "migrant laborer" (Case, "Playing in the Lesbian Workshop").

contemporary American artists with a clear analysis about class issues. She's quick to point out inequities in the distribution of resources for those who make their lives in the theater. She still lives in the rent-controlled apartment on the Lower East Side of Manhattan that she has leased since the late 1970s, but Shaw and Weaver now also own a small plot of land in upstate New York that has become a haven for them and a small community of other lesbian friends and artists.

Around 1999, Shaw finally bought the Airstream trailer for which she always longed and acquired a laptop computer in 2004 after Weaver posted an Internet appeal on Shaw's sixtieth birthday to her friends and admirers. But Shaw's wealth comes in different forms than the cold currency of cash. Her story exemplifies a generation of politically committed, artistically daring feminist and lesbian artists who never compromised, who never excised the lesbian or feminist cant of their work so they could apply for grants or be acceptable in more traditional terms. Shaw has always been committed to the labor of building community, to being a cultural worker with a way of life that provides a model for aspiring artists who care deeply about the world and its future. She and Weaver founded the WOW Café, the now infamous women's performance space and collective that still makes its home on Manhattan's East 4th Street in a nearly abandoned building that they eventually negotiated to buy from the city. Shaw recalls that in the beginning she did "a lot of labor there. I washed the floors there for like five or six years. . . . I came every morning before I'd go to work or wherever. I went to make sure the floors were clean. . . . It was a real pleasure to have my own theater and wash the floors."

In the story Shaw tells about how she was first thrust into performing alone, colleagues at Hampshire College called to ask Shaw and Weaver to come to central Massachusetts to perform *Lesbians Who Kill*. Weaver was working in London at the time and wasn't available, but on impulse Shaw told the organizers that she had a solo show she could bring instead. "They said, 'What's it called?' I said, 'What's the show for?' They said, 'Parents and Friends Week-end.' I said, 'It's called *You're Just Like My Father.*' So I had three months to make it over the summer and did it in the fall. I had all my friends direct it with me; Stacy Makishi, Karena Rahall, and Stormy [Brandenberger] helped, too. . . . That's how I started doing solo. I called it *You're Just Like My Father* 'cause women at WOW would say that to me all the time." The serendipity of the invitation, the spontaneity of the title, and the reversed order of naming the show and then making it became characteristic of Shaw's work. She loves the pressure of a deadline and the assignment of making a piece for an occasion.

Performing Gender, History, and Memory

Shaw's solo performances form a body of autobiographical work intimately tied to the history of her flesh. But they also engage key terms in lesbian, feminist, and queer discourse about private and public permutations of gender, sexuality, and race. Her work circulates as part of the public record through discussions among spectators and fans, in articles and essays by critics and scholars, and through the generations of queer artists she has inspired with her work, all of whom want to address the problematics of identity Shaw explores. *You're Just Like My Father* addressed in visceral, performative ways what scholar Judith Halberstam later described as "female masculinity" (1998). What Shaw expected to be a show about gender passing—that is, being a woman who was presumed, in public, to be a man—became a meditation about her relationship with her mother, in which clothing becomes both an object of exchange between them and the sartorial sign of Shaw's alterity. The show's primary visual image is of Shaw binding her breasts and wrapping her hands, wearing boxer shorts, and preparing her body and her psyche for a fight with unseen forces both present and past.

Her second solo show, *Menopausal Gentleman*, also uses clothing as its central image, in an extended contemplation of what it means to be a gentleman going through menopause. The show was occasioned by a 1940s-style suit that had been made for Shaw when she performed as a female musician passing as male—a story based on the life of Billy Tipton—in an uptown production of Carson Kreitzer's play *Slow Drag* at American Place Theatre in 1996. In what became her most influential performance, that suit provided the *gestus* for Shaw's carefully crafted masculinity in *Menopausal Gentleman*—she shot the cuffs, adjusted the pants, pulled at the jacket tails, and straightened the collar, proudly smoothing and settling into the costume of a then fifty-four-year-old grandmother passing as a thirty-five-year-old man. In her third solo piece, *To My Chagrin*, Shaw contemplates the legacy of her female masculinity for her biracial "grand-companion-son," Ian. In *Chagrin*, Shaw performs her masculinity through an attachment to cars and the music that plays on their radios, African American blues and propulsive rock and roll. The songs send her—in perhaps her most physical performance—dancing across the hood of a rusty old Chevy truck that provides the show's set piece, rolling under its chassis, and finally sitting in potent stillness behind its wheel.

Shaw's solos follow Split Britches' method of devising performances improvisationally, beginning with themes that express her emotional, personal, and political insights and experiences. She still works closely with Weaver, who often directs, edits, or generally consults on Shaw's work, and with choreographer Stormy Brandenberger to create movement vocabularies that require a powerful grace. Her performances are blocked almost like musical numbers, building by accretion in short bits, even shorter throwaway lines, or longer, more elegiac contemplations, typically about longing and loss. Shaw balances a kind of stand-up comic patter with a poet's heart and style. The performances avoid the essentialisms of psychology; little "happens" in them. Instead, she weaves stories cut through with recorded music and refers to politics, world events, and people's capacity to love, as well as harm, each other.

Scholar Sue-Ellen Case calls Shaw's writing "butch haiku." As *A Menopausal Gentleman* makes so evident, Shaw writes her plays across the page in a vibrant mix of poetry and prose that captures the bumpy but smooth, rough yet elegant rhythm of her speech. Shaw's solo shows move in fits and starts, accumulating images and actions, roaming a register from loud to soft, manic to contemplative. Her refusal to conform to well-made-play conventions, or even to the nonlinearity of by now well-established postmodern forms, makes her performances as hybrid as her gender presentations offstage.

Shaw's publicity photos immediately establish her ambiguous, hybrid gender style. The signal image for *You're Just Like My Father* is of Shaw wearing boxer shorts and standing boxer style, with her breasts bound, her shoulders and middle bare, taping her fist with an elastic bandage while she looks out at the viewer in a sexy dare. For *Menopausal Gentleman,* the semiotically rich image shows Shaw's body in close-up from the neck down to the groin. Her breasts are full and bare and rest on her belly above a belt holding up pin-striped men's pants. Shaw's hand is shoved through the pants' open zipper, and her fingers wriggle. The image dares anyone to call a masculine woman an imitation man. By filling that zipper with her own hand, Shaw both illustrates lesbian sexual practices and parodies what is stereotyped as lesbian lack (as in the perennial and pernicious, "What do lesbians do in bed?"). In the publicity image for Shaw's Austin performance of *To My Chagrin,* she sits on the old truck's hood in a country setting, looking off behind her shoulder into the trees. She wears a light 1950s-style suit that softens her image. Sharing the frame is her grandson, who was then seven years old. Ian wears red shorts and no top, and his bare, dark skin contrasts richly with Shaw's whiteness. They sit companionably.

Even these marketing images evoke the magnetism of Shaw's presence. She very much wants to be liked by audiences. She remarks that in Hot Peaches, "[W]e were all just too saucy for our own good. . . . Lois really taught me subtlety . . . [which is necessary] if you want the audience to like you and stay for the show." For Shaw, allowing "people to see that someone who looks and acts like me is a generous kind of funny person" is very much an embodied political act. In *Menopausal Gentleman,* for instance, she moves into the audience several times during the performance, working the house like a lounge singer, shaking people's hands, touching their shoulders, looking into their eyes, and singing them a phrase or two of her reinterpretation of the song "My Way." Spectators who connect with Shaw in one of these moments find it a stunning exchange, at once deeply intimate yet utterly public, given that it happens within the show's theatrical frame.

A bittersweet inheritance haunts Shaw's work. In *You're Just Like My Father,* she recalls that her father had a "heart condition; he had to count to ten before he hit us." Later, as Shaw, the metaphorical butch boxer, strides to the center of the boxing ring to speak into the overhead microphone, she says she, too, counts down from ten before she acts. In *Menopausal Gentleman,* Shaw spins mournful, melancholic, piercing tales about the passage of time playing over and within a female body lived in a masculine style for which biology provides a kind of necessary historical referent. *To My Chagrin* wrestles with Shaw's attempt to create a living past to hand down to Ian. Rather than letting biology and culture chart their course, she works to refashion for him lessons about what it means to be a man while she acknowledges the difference her whiteness makes in navigating her own route through culture: "I'm blinded by morning / I'm blinded white / It's bright, it's white / So much white in my head."

Shaw's performances thoughtfully chart the intersections of gender and sexuality, race and class. In a generation in which lesbians and trans men take pleasure in stretching the envelope of conventional masculinity and queer communities engage politically and socially with transgender identity and style, Shaw's longtime performance as a masculine woman provides a cherished role model. In fact, Shaw's performances of a complex combination of femininity and masculinity preceded contemporary transgender political activism and theorizing, making her in some ways the "butch hero" who came to model, for many trans folk, the potential of refusing biological gender assignments.[4]

Shaw's relationship with Weaver helped to recuperate butch-femme style from the dustbin of feminism.[5] Lesbians who engaged in gender play—especially those who adopted masculine personal performance styles either from economic necessity or from erotic preference (or both)—were rejected by the second wave of American liberal feminism and forced into the closet to keep them from alienating the mainstream acceptance this brand of feminism courted. As Shaw says in *You're Just Like My Father*, "Feminists made me hate dolphins, I mean dildos. / They tried to make me hate boxer shorts." She details how the objects that signified female masculinity were verboten in lesbian and feminist culture of the 1970s and 1980s because of their association with men. As a result, Shaw says, "I didn't really learn from feminism. . . . I learned from the bars." Whereas lesbian feminism of the 1970s forbade the adoption of the masculine styles of 1950s lesbian culture, ably documented by Elizabeth Lapovsky Kennedy and Madeline D. Davis in *Boots of Leather, Slippers of Gold* (1993), the early 1990s saw a resurgence of butch-femme activity. Shaw and Weaver lived well ahead of this theatrical and political curve, performing and conducting their daily lives as gender outlaws at a time when feminism's prohibition against masculinity and its disparagement of the "femme" made their social and personal performances vanguard practices onstage and off.

By the beginning of the twenty-first century, however, butch-femme gender had been overshadowed by a new emphasis on what Halberstam theorized as female masculinity. Drag kings took to the stage, women who used artificial facial hair, costumes, and accessories to signify masculinity and lip-synced to rock and hip-

---

4. See, for example, Anderson Toone's "Drag King Timeline" at his Web site, http://anderson toone.com/timeline/dktimeline.html, in which Shaw's solo performances and her performances with Weaver and Split Britches appear throughout the thirty-year history he covers as significant and influential.

5. See Case, "Toward a Butch-Femme Aesthetic," where this history is explicated and theorized.

hop soundtracks to secure an association with racially subaltern cultures. They played to audiences of newly minted "queers," who appreciated the drag kings' appropriations of masculinity and its various idioms just as people who called themselves queer had tried to resignify the derogatory slur of an earlier generation. Where the gender revisions Shaw and Weaver promoted in performance had been staged in theaters like the WOW Café, PS122, Dixon Place, and other venues in New York City and in performance spaces around the country, drag kings produced their shows in bars and clubs and at conferences and festivals like the International Drag KingCommunity Extravaganza (see www.idke.info/), moving gender performance farther away from the theater scene and the lesbian communities in which Shaw made her initial impression.[6] At the same time, a new trans discourse began to dominate many U.S. lesbian subcultures. People who once adopted butch lesbian monikers became more comfortable with "transman" to represent their refusal of traditional binary gender assignments, and many employed the American medical establishment and pharmaceutical companies to more closely conform their flesh to their felt genders, using surgeries and hormones to reassign their sex to the one that felt more comfortable and "natural."[7]

Throughout this movement, Shaw has remained committed to her historical identity as a butch lesbian. "I never felt like I wanted to be a man, ever," Shaw admits, "even though they consider me the father of the trans movement." By her own testimony, she's been a role model to many trans men and female-to-male transsexuals, for whom she feels much respect and empathy. "[T]o change from a woman's name to a man's name . . . it's a lot of work. And I'm willing to do the work if that's what they want. It's totally up to people what they want to be called. . . . I have to keep alert and respectful of what they want," she says. Shaw counters claims from some quarters, saying, "[A] lot of women think it's real trendy

---

6. See Ji Hye for an explication of this historical shift.
7. See Salamon for an elaboration of transgender identity and an astute argument against some of its implicit essentialisms.

to be a tranny. It's really hard. And it's really painful. . . . I think sometimes in politics we think we know everything. But we don't know everybody." In *To My Chagrin*, she says, "Thank God with this amount of testosterone I'll never have balls." Shaw says, "[P]art of me is mourning; where are the butches going? . . . A lot of my friends are boys now." Shaw has remained identified with her own foundational brand of female masculinity, always complicating the combination of genders across her body and her performances but never willing to forgo the one for the other. In fact, female biology is inescapable in Shaw's performances, keeping her poised within complex gendered contradictions. She's suffered the indignities of being female her entire life with irony, wit, intelligence, and love. Rather than modifying or rejecting her female body, she respects its power.

In *Menopausal Gentleman*, for example, Shaw performs as a mannerly middle-class and middle-aged man, but the show describes her struggle with female hormonal changes, on which she casts a new, queer light. Far from romanticizing her changing biology, Shaw celebrates using up all of her eggs—"They say women have a certain amount of eggs to use up in a lifetime. I DID IT!"—rather than mourning the end of her fertility. But she keeps her female parts close to her masculine side, exemplifying how a "female man"—the figure feminist novelist Joanna Russ once described—can swing back and forth among them. Shaw constructs her masculinity with care and affection and an ironic self-love: "Gotta get the sound coming from my chest, I have to concentrate to keep my voice low, to match my suit. / Otherwise when I open my mouth to speak it's like what happened when movies went from silents to talkies and actors lost their jobs 'cause their voices didn't match their bodies." This honest, open attention to performative detail distinguishes Shaw from other trans or butch lesbian performers who hide the physical marks of their femaleness to pass as male.

Shaw's masculinity is so deeply ingrained and lightly worn that she doesn't perseverate on "the pass" that preoccupies many other trans performers. Instead, both and multiple genders cohabit in Shaw's work. In *Menopausal Gentleman,* she boasts, "I was born Butch. / I didn't learn it at theater school. . . . I'm so queer I don't even have to talk about it; it speaks for itself." The deep seriousness of her gendered situation as a lived state ("It's not funny," she insists in *Menopausal Gentleman.* "An older woman being a gentleman is not funny") preoccupies Shaw more than what other people think. She says, "I had never really tried to pass in my life. I had always been mistaken for a man, but I had never passed," enumerating a crucial difference between intention and reception. Passing becomes multiple and metaphorical in Shaw's work. In *Menopausal Gentleman,* for instance, she is "trying to pass as a person when there is a beast inside of me, a beast on fire who waits in the shadows of the night."

Shaw's difference from many people in the trans community hinges in part on the class preoccupations of her own performance of masculinity. Shaw has said that a lot of people who become trans men refashion themselves as working-class men.[8] Shaw says she doesn't really understand why they romanticize that figure; she has always seen herself as a gentleman. Shaw ironizes her masculinity, where other trans men appear earnest in their gender impersonations and want very much to pass as men.[9] They assume working-class identities to secure their masculine authenticity, rejecting the potentially effete performances of the male middle class. Shaw, however, isn't afraid of playing the gentleman. Perhaps because she was born and has lived most of her life as a working-class person, performance lets her assume an upwardly mobile gender identity.

In addition, in some of her work with Weaver and Split Britches, Shaw played female roles, which also distinguishes her from drag kings and trans men. Watching her perform in women's clothing in a revival of *Dress Suits to Hire,* in Austin, Texas, in 2005,

---

8. See, for example, Leslie Feinberg, Loren Cameron, and Max Wolf Valerio.
9. This notion was suggested by Case in her interview with Dolan and Pryor on 15 April 2005.

for example, you could see Shaw undoing femininity because her masculinity kept seeping into the interstices of her performance. She says:

> My wearing a dress is like playing a drag queen. . . . I was always butch, but I played on that. . . . But that's why I got an Obie for *Dress Suits*. It was because all of a sudden the person who played James Dean all the time was playing Rita Hayworth and there was a little magic. . . . Drag is . . . a magic trick. It's what people love. They love boys dressing up as girls. They don't love girls dressing up as boys so much. But now they're getting used to it.

Shaw's gendered transformations are intimately tied to the costumes she wears in each of her performances. But unlike gender illusionists—which might describe many drag queens, drag kings, and even some trans men—Shaw often dresses and undresses in front of her audiences, constructing and deconstructing the signs of gender in real time and theatrical space. In *You're Just Like My Father,* for example, she begins bare breasted, wearing boxer shorts and sitting in front of a suitcase, from which she removes one Ace bandage, which she uses to wrap her breasts, and then another to encase her fist. Later in the performance, she dresses in an army uniform, which she soon replaces with a silky robe, the more casual, sexual costume of a man of leisure. Later still, she replaces the robe with a suit, ending the performance by saluting and leaving with the suitcase, carrying the baggage of gender that represents both her choices and her burdens.

In *Menopausal Gentleman,* Shaw's beautiful suit almost becomes another character, an outfit that both liberates and imprisons her, the battleground on which the skirmish between biological hormones and self-performance rages. Continuing her contemplation of gendered clothing in *To My Chagrin,* Shaw opens with a remark about the musician Sam Cooke, who was "killed in his underwear in a motel room. / Did you hear that? / I know he wore white boxer shorts." Boxer shorts offer a point of identification between Shaw and Cooke, as they haunt her own masculinity. But later in *To My Chagrin*, she unbuttons her starched white shirt so that a video of Ian dancing can be projected onto her bare white breasts, placing the little boy metaphorically in her heart, at the center of her female masculinity. Few performers risk physical and emotional vulnerability as masterfully as Shaw. Her willingness to bare her breasts in a performance that explores her masculinity through her relationship to cars and music exemplifies her refusal to be pinned down to a fixed, stable gender representation.

As constructed as her female masculinity has been throughout her performance career and her life, Shaw has always testified to her profound connection to the body and the flesh. As early as *You're Just Like My Father,* Shaw connected blood to a carnal femaleness, as a volcanic or vampiric force but also as the quotidian clots of menses moving through her. In *You're Just Like My Father,* she says, "When I see blood, I want to eat it, chew it up good, or chop it up with onions for chopped liver, put an egg over it and have steak tartare, salt and pepper and some Worcestershire sauce, put it in a blender and add ice for a nice summer drink, a cranberry blood clot or a bloody Mary, but Mary's not here to hold back my hands."

Much of Shaw's work is pedagogical, as she teaches spectators about the pleasures and problems of gender performance. "Men's underwear folds so neatly and square, / Women's underwear doesn't have a real logic to it," she observes in *My Father.* Clothing is totemic for Shaw, reminiscent of gender practices that give her life texture and shape. In *My Father,* she admits that she chose to be a boy so she "could wear starched shirts / To keep the ugly world away from girls, / And so girls could hold my hand / And rest their head on my shoulder, / My clean white shoulder, stiff with pleasure." Shaw's chivalry comes from the sharp insistence of neatly pressed clothes, boasting the razor-edged creases with which they cut through the world. In *Menopausal Gentleman,* Shaw mostly regrets that her "private summer messes up [her] starched shirts. . . . It's hard to be a gentleman in menopause."

Shaw's solo performances often underline her essential melancholy and isolation, even though they're also funny, sardonic, and poignant. "Don't leave me" is a wistful request that echoes through *You're Just Like My Father* and *Menopausal Gentleman*. Shaw says, "You can always count on leaving. Saying goodbye. Saying hello, saying goodbye. My friend JR, from the country where me and Lois have our cabin, she goes, 'You're here, you leave. You're here, you leave. That's what you do. Sometimes you're here and then you go away.'" Although such comings and goings might represent the existential condition of any itinerant performer, Shaw's plays demonstrate that she has never quite resigned herself to their inevitable, repeating cycle. *Gentleman* ends by describing how "[g]oodbyes dribble out of my mouth. I drool on the sidewalk after you're gone. They'll find me here years later, they'll find me yelling and waving through the trucks and the busses, and the cars and the traffic, over and over, joining all the spirits they walt disneyed over in Times Square." Shaw remains frozen there, waving good-bye to a lover who won't return her gaze, mingling with the spirits of the gay male sex culture whose exiled denizens Samuel Delany evokes in *Times Square Red, Times Square Blue*. Shaw remains liminal, both inside and out, on the threshold of hello and good-bye.

A Trilogy of Female Masculinity

In *You're Just Like My Father*, Shaw considers the legacy of family and relationships that have brought her to the brink of the boxing ring in which she stages her contest with the dominant culture. "I thought [the show] was going to be about passing as a man," Shaw recalls about her first solo show, but "it was all about becoming my mother's lover, sort of." The performance details the legacy of her mother's mixed messages. One on hand, she prized Shaw's resemblance to her husband and dressed her in his clothes. "Do you know you look just like your father? You remind me of him. Do you want a pair of his cuff links? . . . How about a tie?" Shaw's mother asked. "I dressed in my mother's memories," Shaw recalls in *My Father.* On the other hand, Shaw's mother threatened her with hell: "[D]on't let your sisters see you. . . . I don't want them dressing like that, and I worry about you, that you're going to hell because of the way you dress, eternal hell to burn with the devil. And I don't want you bringing your sisters with you." Shaw's mother seduces her with accoutrements of masculinity that carry an erotic charge for both of them and then she damns Shaw for how she dresses. Her mother at once gives Shaw her desire and curses it.

The show draws from Shaw's family history. Her grandfather was an Irish boxer and fruit seller in a Boston market, who knocked out Joe Lewis when Lewis stole fruit from his stall. "That's what I heard," Shaw says. "[I]t doesn't even matter if it's true or not." That family history of combative protectiveness haunts all of Shaw's performances. "I think I'm a really protective person," she says. "I like to nurture people and keep them safe." (Shaw calls herself "a halfway house for lesbians.") That fierce protectiveness became emblematic for many trans men. Shaw's relationship with her own body modeled a kind of pride; she describes "trusting . . . my body, to wrap it. I hadn't seen anybody wrap their body in public. . . . First I wrap my breasts, then I wrap my hands. Then I'm safe. The wrappings become my safety." Seeing Shaw's photos from *You're Just Like My Father* prominently featured in alternative newspapers—a "wrapped lesbian on the cover"—was a big deal for some of the trans men with whom she associated at the time.

"Once a shrink asked me where my desire comes from. / I said, 'From my hands.'" Shaw also admits in *My Father,* "I associate everything with cars" (an association she would draw out in *To My Chagrin*) "except my sexuality I attribute to my hands." Rather than the phallic primacy of masculinity, Shaw's desire and sexuality abide in her hands, even though, as she charts the cartography of desire in *You're Just Like My Father,* "The man I am today still thinks all desire starts at the mouth. It comes from right inside the lip, the inside part of the lips that are always moist." Although her body might be confined in elastic bandages and attired in a masculine style, her flesh responds to longing from a wet, feminine place, beginning with the tender skin inside the lips. *You're Just Like My Father* lays out Shaw's sexuality and her desire like a dare: "It doesn't matter if you believe anything I say or not," she shrugs early in the performance. These are her truths. Where and how they land on some fundamental level isn't her problem.

Her second solo show, *Menopausal Gentleman*, showcases Shaw in an impeccably cut 1940s style pin-striped suit, but her gentleman is far from decorous and reserved. On a nearly bare stage, she physicalizes the contradictions of suffering the "tiger" of menopause in a body whose masculinity orders her exterior. She bounds across the space, snapping the sleeves of her suit, settling herself into the crotch of her pants, pulling at the knotted tie that soaks up the sweat her hormones send coursing down her neck. The performance masterfully embodies the battle between hormones and heart, the frisson between Shaw's performance of herself and the implacable dictates of her body's chemistry.

Shaw's presence in *Menopausal Gentleman* is more refined and sophisticated than the boxer's rough-and-ready dare in *You're Just Like My Father*. She performs as a masculine woman who has come to terms with her mother's interdiction and has internalized as the hellfire of menopause the damnation her mother promised. The irony for a middle-aged female gentleman, of course, is her inability to avoid the hormonal storms of the change of life. But the performance documents how Shaw lives with her contradictory state. The gentleman trying so hard to maintain the press of his starched shirts pushes himself to accept how aging changes everything and nothing. Shaw tells the audience, "This body is inside this suit. This suit will give you an idea of what I feel like. Inside I'm all strapped down 'cause you can't have a great suit like this and have bumps on the outside." She smooths the bumps of femininity to keep them from upsetting the lines of her suit, but she's not afraid of a harsher light of scrutiny: "I want to be loved in this light that shows the lumps in my legs and the stretch marks on my belly, 'cause then I'll know I've been loved." To love Shaw is to accept her contradictions—the bumps pressed into invisibility by the elastic wound around her chest still remain part of her flesh.

Shaw's struggle between her body's internal female chemistry and the sober, collected, masculine exterior she prefers forms the central agon of *Menopausal Gentleman*. One of the show's scenes depicts a relaxation exercise in which Shaw lays herself out center stage on the bench that provides the show's only set piece. She cajoles her limbs to calm down, to fall into the elusive sleep for which she's desperate. Almost in a parody of actor warm-ups that require a systematic check of musculature, she assesses each of her body's zones: "Okay, throat, that's a hard one, my throat, everything is jammed up in my throat," lightly referring to the emotions that knot in her trachea. The exercise fails; her brain refuses to relax, as regrets and worries trip through her veins. She obsesses over her lack of health insurance and her poor performance as a mother ("[I]t was the '70s," she reassures herself, "no one was a good mother in the '70s."), until finally, she leaps up from the bench, yelling, "I give up . . . EVERYBODY UP!" banging on and reawakening each of her body's parts. The moment is typical of Shaw's mordant humor, which erupts suddenly and physically in all of her work. As she hits herself repeatedly, she seems to have adapted a Marx Brothers routine as a solo. Later in *Gentleman,* as her hormones begin to assert their control, she spirals into hysteria, accompanied by Screamin' Jay Hawkins's "I Put a Spell on You." The song ends with Shaw wearing her suit jacket backward, her arms sticking out of the reversed sleeves like frantic signals, while her large feet, clad in men's brogans and the white socks of the 1950s greaser, skip madly in time to a beat that commands her.

Shaw's emotional and sartorial inspirations run to male figures of the 1940s. Jimmy Cagney and James Dean recur frequently as icons of American popular culture who provide her role models, along with the African American jazz and blues musicians—Nina Simone, Barry White, Sam Cooke, Chuck Berry, Otis Redding, and James Brown among them—who provide the soundtrack for her life and her performances. Contemporary lesbian culture appears fake and plastic to Shaw. ("The only thing I liked about *Desert Hearts* was when she went backwards really fast in her truck," Shaw scoffs, citing the first widely popular lesbian film, directed by Donna Deitch in 1985, in which the lesbian heroine begins courting her straight woman love interest by driving in reverse down a Las Vegas desert highway next to the car that brings the woman to town.) But the heroes and antiheroes of popular culture can't help Shaw grapple with the complications of her own life. As Shaw describes falling to pieces in the night in *Gentleman,* she complains, "Marlon Brando was not there for me. James Dean failed to come through, where was Susan Hayward when I needed her, and Rita Hayworth was nowhere to be found."

Haunting this grievance is the history of performances in which Shaw quoted these figures: she famously played Stanley (a role Brando made famous on film) to Weaver's Stella in *Belle Reprieve* (1991), the queering of *Streetcar Named Desire* mounted by Shaw, Weaver, and the gay men of the London-based Bloolips troupe. Shaw quotes Dean's smoldering sexuality in many of her roles, and in *Dress Suits to Hire,* Shaw resembled Hayworth, playing opposite Weaver's Hayward, who sounded femme accompaniments to Shaw's butch bass lines. But the gendered examples of popular culture finally fail Shaw. She writes her reinterpretations of gender and sexuality across a body that both refuses and embraces a biological root. She wears her gestures as light quotations of a history of gender styles, cloaking flesh etched by moving through a culture that can't quite read her citations.

Menopausal Gentleman poses the existential questions absurdism has long worried: Who are "you"? Will you come get me? Will you return? To whom is Shaw really speaking, out of the man-sized collar of her suit as her bound breasts press down on her chest? Who will save Shaw? Who is even there, which, as theater theorist Herb Blau has suggested, addresses the primary condition of theater: Who's there? Who's talking? Who's watching? Who's listening?[10] In postmodern lesbian queer performance, the question is embellished: Who's there to catch you, to desire you, to see your complexities as your performance of your body rewrites gender and sexuality, class and race?

To My Chagrin uses the occasion of Shaw's grandson's life to continue her meditations on the burdens of history and her responsibility to the future. Ian stirs Shaw's understanding of how her biological bloodlines and her cultural kinship structures intersect. *Chagrin* details Shaw's desire to share her knowledge of what it means to be a man with Ian, to reach him across the boundaries of history and race and culture, to help him navigate his own manhood. In the performance, she uses the cab of a decrepit truck to strike poses, sitting behind its wheel, bounding through its open bed, and interacting with percussionist Vivian Stoll, who shares the stage with her and plays her drum set from the old truck's bed, cut off from the cab and perched across the way. Stoll punctuates Shaw's stories and responds to her narrative needs, playing the performance as a duet, as well as a nearly archival engagement with the songbook of American blues and jazz. As Margo Jefferson writes in her *New York Times* review of *To My Chagrin*:

Ms. Shaw has the virile physicality of [Sinatra, Jerry Lee Lewis, and Otis Redding]. She has her own choreographer, too—she and Stormy Brandenberger do each other proud. She hurls herself against the Chevy as if it were a guitar she was out to decimate. She sits inside it in the classic cool-guy way: window down, head out, tough expression, arm resting on the chassis with easy possessiveness. That's the attitude she brings to a brief disquisition on masculinity, too. Yes, she looks masculine, she says, coming out from under the car. What exactly does that mean? . . . By the end of . . . *To My Chagrin*, . . . Ms. Shaw has turned the question Henry Higgins posed in "My Fair Lady" on its self-satisfied head. "Why can't a

---

10. See Blau.

woman be more like a man?" the professor asked. Watching Ms. Shaw makes us ask: "Why can't white soul men be more like this woman?"

In *To My Chagrin* her grandson represents a new companionship. Shaw anticipates her father/son grandmama/grand-companion-son relationship with Ian, who's born prematurely, a "pretty shade of lilac. . . . A lilac baby with leopard upholstery and / Mixed / Race stripes / Racing stripes / Mixed spots / On your rear end." Pressing the automotive metaphor, Shaw croons, "My premature grand baby lilac son! / You came flying out of your mama's garage / Right onto my wrong side of the road." Ian's birth brings a new sense of urgency to Shaw's ruminations on masculinity, race, and class. He opens a new world for Shaw, as she contemplates how his mixed-race and her mixed-gender lives offer unique pleasures and pain. Race and gender run parallel here, aspects of Shaw and Ian that don't fit neatly into the dominant imaginary, that require cautious care as these split selves navigate cultural interstates. Shaw compares herself to Ian: "I'm pale I'm all white next to you / I pale in comparison / I'm an inbred white bread / Except for my brown left arm hanging out the car window / From driving right close to the sun."

That brown arm marks her as surely as his African American genes mark Ian, yet Shaw's brownness comes from how she performs her gender, driving like a man with her arm crooked across the car's threshold. Her brownness, then, also represents her butchness, the emblem of how her choice of gender performance makes Shaw mixed, too. Shaw experiments with performances of gender throughout the script, enacting for Ian the complexities of being in the world as a "mixed" person. She revels in the ways her condition can't be resolved, using language to evoke a world turned upside down yet delightful: "And I noticed my hair had grown—/ Short on the sides," she says, speaking in rhythms and patterns that disrupt the expected and replace it with images set askew to the world as it is.

In some ways, *Chagrin* is a journal for Ian that he might read to learn something about his future. As Shaw says in *You're Just Like My Father,* "My mother said, 'Every word you speak is forever in the air, it will never go away.' She meant it as a threat to keep me from saying bad things, but I took it as a convenient sort of a diary. . . . It's only now that I realize that these words can be used against me." "I have been accused of being masculine / I would like to talk to you about that. / About passing on my masculinity," she says in *Chagrin.* She fears for Ian. Translating her own painful ostracism from feminism and early lesbian culture into the risk that he will be racially profiled in a racist state, she tries to teach him how to be a man of color in a world that could kill him: "If you move you're over / You could die if you move. / You could be killed for moving. / Don't reach for anything you could be killed for." Shaw knows that sometimes how you're seen has nothing to do with what you're really reaching for or who you really are. Sometimes, your interaction with culture—if you're a person of color like Ian or a butch grandmama like Shaw—just makes you a screen for other people's projections. When Shaw, later in the performance, bares her breasts as a projection screen for video footage of Ian playing, she replaces cultural presumption with an image of what she truly carries in her heart.

Cars are the props of Shaw's dreams in *Chagrin.* She rattles off the name, make, and year of every vehicle she ever owned and takes pride in knowing how they work and how she looks sitting behind their steering wheels. The automobile supplies Shaw with an all-American image of movement, pioneering adventure, class mobility, ownership, and gender dominance, as music blares through car speakers into shared air. But the vehicle for these dreams in *To My Chagrin* is a broken-down, immobile, machine-cut Chevy pickup truck that Shaw shares onstage with Stoll. Shaw uses the truck's cab to sit, posing and musing. She dances over its roof, over the hood, underneath the chassis, rolling on a dolly that lets her skid in and out from its lowest depths. Stoll sits anchored by her drum set in the truck's bed, placed across the stage, where she punctuates Shaw's narrative. Occasionally, Stoll joins Shaw by the truck's cab. The simple fact of Stoll's presence and the two women's companionship makes Shaw seem less alone than in her previous solo performances. Instead of the ubiquitous, plaintive plea, "Don't leave me," which Shaw addresses to old lovers, friends, and even the audiences of her two earlier performances, *To My Chagrin* is textured with Shaw's camaraderie with Stoll and the absent Ian and her determination to make these relationships work. Stoll's presence anchors Shaw and gives her another center of energy off of which to bounce her vitality and her mourning for a past that recedes further, daily.

To My Chagrin, in fact, concerns the passage of time even more than Shaw's two earlier solo performances collected here. She begins the piece by reporting on various jazz and blues musicians of color who have long since died, like Bessie Smith or Billie Holiday (Shaw can't remember which), "dying because they wouldn't treat her at a white only / Hospital emergency room." Mortality haunts *Chagrin,* as Shaw contemplates the living and the dead. One of the performance's most potent metaphors comes with the story of a 150-year-old tree that crashes to the ground in a thunderstorm, smashing across six backyards and leaving a gaping hole in the sky, "where it had been for so long," and in the earth. She describes how she crawled, naked, into the hole, burying herself in the dirt, joining herself to the elements in a way that cleansed her even as it reminded her that she's ever closer to her own demise. "I'm mature now and I'm dirty," she reports. "Just from living. / And graying at the temples. . . . Time flies, then you go back to the silence you came from / Before you were born. Where was that now? / Oh, yeah. Down with the roots of the trees. / Quiet like when. . . . / You turn off the ignition after a long hard drive." This resonant image joins the car to the earth, silence to the grave, not ominously, but with a potent sense of hope. Watching Shaw sit in the cab, you can imagine the car settling into itself, pinging now and then as it simmers down, the driver waiting a moment before leaving, feeling her parts release and realign themselves just like the truck. The moment encompasses the past, the present, and the future. Shaw lingers, patient in this connection with life tinged with death, a beginning haunted by an end.

Partly because the truck and Stoll give Shaw multiple points from which to move and return, her performance in *Chagrin* is more fully physical and active, more spatially rich and focused. The old truck is an animated, expressive third partner in Shaw's journey. As she dances on, around, and with it throughout *Chagrin*, "The truck seems alive with lights coming from inside and underneath as Peggy crashes and dives." She uses "the door like a guitar and a dance partner," tapping into her masculinity to cozy up to the truck's steel skeleton like a lover. The totemic quality of the truck and her companionate onstage relationship with Stoll—who wears her own gender performance lightly, appearing slightly masculine but at the same time more feminine than Shaw—allows Shaw's sharp ruminations to pop from the stage. With Stoll along, *Chagrin* treats Shaw kindly; at one point, the stage directions indicate, Stoll "climbs out of the truck bed, comes up behind Peggy and wraps her jacket around her shoulders." This moment of care and concern, of touch and connection, between two women coded as butch seems staged somewhere outside of the dictates of a binary gender system since their performed masculinity doesn't preclude physical intimacy between them, as it might in a more conventional performance of gender.

The hole in the earth made by the tree, on the other hand, calls Shaw back to something embodied and female. Crawling into it as Ian watches—for, she says, "How could I pass up this opportunity of a hole?"—she senses her own transformation into something elemental: "I think it was the way I took my clothes off combined with / The shock of the tree falling that alerted you that / Something had changed. / With no clothes, and through your eyes, my body felt / Very feminine, very soft and very naked." As she rests in the hole in the ground, she describes "[j]ust my head appearing to the world where the tree had been," filling the sudden vacuum left by nature. Buried in the earth, she feels the soil leach from her the inescapable toxins of life above ground, until finally an unidentified "you" digs her out with its hands, crying, "It's a girl, a big butch girl, you yelled to the fallen / Tree and my old Torino and the fire. The tree died and you / Lived! You said. The tree sacrificed itself for you!" The "you" in *Chagrin* vacillates between Shaw and Ian, the spectator and Stoll, charting a constellated kinship structure with Shaw at its center, cleansed by rituals of death and rebirth that leave her finally freed, lighter, connected, born, like Ian, into a world made different by her presence.

Must—The Inside Story

You're Just Like My Father, Menopausal Gentleman, and *To My Chagrin* comprise Shaw's trilogy about masculinity. *Must—The Inside Story: A Journey through the Shadows of a City, a Pound of Flesh, a Book of Love,* her collaboration with Suzy Willson of the U.K.-based Clod Ensemble, begins a new chapter for Shaw, following more closely the theme of aging and embodiment that begins to surface more forcefully toward the trilogy's end. In *Must,* which closes the collection of performances gathered here, Shaw's meditations on aging and loss take on an even more melancholic, elegiac tone. The epigraph is from Ovid's *The Metamorphoses:* "Our bodies are ceaselessly changing. What we were yesterday and are today, we will not be tomorrow." The quotation could represent all of Shaw's work, as her performances chart her personal transformations in the public forum of theater. But with *Must,* Shaw traces the remainders of aging, challenging this time the binary of inside/outside through which our bodies are typically parsed.

Architecturally sculpted light frames specific parts of Shaw's body throughout the performance. In one instance, she puts her face in a sharp white square projected against a column; in another, she's crossed by bars of light as if sun is forcing its way between the slats of a venetian blind. With her features brilliantly lit, she delivers snippets of narrative that appraise her career-long preoccupations. "I keep finding the future inside of me," she muses.

"There are different ways of seeing inside me," she suggests. "You could guess what's in here. / You could x-ray me. / You could touch me. / Or you could believe what I tell you." In the earlier performance trilogy gathered in this collection, Shaw invited the audience to do all of these things as a way of seeing into the stuff of which she's made.

As in *To My Chagrin, Must* moves toward an investigation of Shaw's insides, as slides of capillaries and blood vessels project over her bare back. She removes her shirt here not to offer her heart as a home for her grand-companion-son, but to turn her skin inside out, to confuse the borders of a body that is always reveling in such stunning, intentional disarray. Shaw becomes in these moments the beautiful object of her own art. She directs more of her boundless, inchoate love inward toward herself than outward, as if she's reconciled with her own need for care and attention. Her clavicles, she thinks, are her most beautiful part. And yet as slides of veins and tissues are projected behind her, while Shaw stands on a step unit downstage center, watching them go by, spectators know that her beauty isn't confined to just those particular bones. The slides project the insides of a body (which may or may not be hers—its authenticity doesn't in the end matter) artfully, and the gallery-like space of the New York Shakespeare Festival's Public Theatre, where Shaw presented *Must* during the Under the Radar Festival in January 2010, heightened the analogy of the body to a painting.

Must was created as part of the Clod Ensemble's Performing Medicine program and toured to medical schools and theaters around the world. The production has the aura of a deeply felt lecture-demonstration in which Shaw's body comes to stand in for all bodies, revising what lesbian theorist Monique Wittig once called the "axis of categorization" by putting a butch lesbian body at the center of an illustration of life. Once again Shaw deconstructs binaries, here of inside/outside and animal/human, comparing herself in *Must*'s prelude to an elephant with thick and ancient skin, experience crafted on its deep and hanging folds.

Must elevates the poetry of Shaw's earlier work and shows off

her enigmatic, evocative writing, backed here by the complemen-
tary sounds of a small band—a violin, piano, and double bass—
that graces its notes off her words. Unlike her lively interaction
with Stoll in *To My Chagrin,* or the exuberant riffing on rock and
roll that styled so much of her locomotion in *Menopausal Gentleman,* Shaw acknowledges the presence of *Must*'s band but keeps
herself separate, her energy distinct. She seems more conscious of
her solitude onstage; her words address her interiority, even as she
projects her/the body's insides out. Under all the gender performance, all the class consciousness and racial mixing to which her
trilogy refers, lies this moving cartography of the body that represents something ineluctable about life itself. "It's a journey
through the shadows of a city," she notes. "A map. The wrinkles on
my face are where the map gets folded over and over." *Must* is an
ode to her body's ravages and triumphs, a tour of its shadows and
secrets. "I have lumps on my forearms and the front of my thighs
where I store my original thoughts," she explains. What others
might describe as flaws she sees as resources.

The stories remain poignant and moving, tales that honor her
history and the lives of friends, like Migdalia Garcia, who "sucks
calcium outta the inside of chicken bones," and carried Shaw to
the emergency room when she fell off a fence and broke her pelvis
and heels. At the hospital, Garcia "stole all the bandages out of the
cabinets and stuffed them in her jacket pockets, to give to her girlfriend to strap down her breasts, so she could pass as a man on the
streets of Brooklyn. . . . Migdalia Garcia. That's her name / Don't
forget it." The story honors the invention of those, like Shaw, who
subvert dominant culture at every turn, repurposing its effects to
their own ends, so that they can pass with relatively less impunity
than they otherwise might.

"What do you think happened?" Shaw repeats again and again,
asking for a challenge to her own interpretation, a mutual remembering of her body and her past. Doors to her interior reveal memories, old family scores that can't be settled or resolved, rooms
haunted by ancient injunctions. "This is the room my mother has

warned me about," Shaw reports as she opens yet another metaphorical door. "Writhing, half-eaten half skeleton corpses, having sex and eating too much, in agony from biblical words like gluttony and fornication and coveting your neighbor's wife." In another room, her mother is throwing kitchen wares at a wall and will require "eleven shock treatments to get her to wash the dishes."

Must is redolent with everything the short word means. Given the production's predominating elephant images, reference to a condition called "musth" (or "must") is also intended later in the play. In musth, periodically experienced by bull elephants, their testosterone levels rise as much as 60 times higher than normal. In addition to prompting aggressive behavior, the hormone makes elephants secrete a thick liquid from their temporal glands. This image inspires an outpouring of epic grief in *Must*. Shaw says, "When elephants are in must tears flow freely from their eyes / I'm crying for you . . . Stuff is leaking out, draining from my eyes, dripping from my holes everywhere / The flood keeps coming; it sweeps me off my feet."

But "must" has other connotations: the imperative of action and the necessity it implies; something essential and required; and perhaps more obliquely but most apt, given Shaw's performance, the pulp and skin of crushed grapes. In this last definition comes the indispensable, vital Shaw, the performer who gives us the juice of her own fermentation, refusing the distinction between the inside and its covering and reveling in the sometimes brutal strength it takes to make them mix.

Pumped by Performance

Weaver says that what makes Shaw such a good actor is that "she thinks whatever she's experiencing right now is the absolute truth. . . . She's so in the moment; she's not reflecting back." Weaver has directed Shaw's performances frequently and fondly. For Shaw, much of the text is derived from the experience of rehearsing and performing, which requires a director to engage with the artist rather than the "play." Shaw constructs her theater scripts much like she constructs her gendered performances—on impulse, responding to what comes at her from a culture in which she fights constantly to carve out her own space and room for others who are also disenfranchised.

In between the full-length performances collected in *A Menopausal Gentleman,* as palate cleansers of a sort, are monologues from Shaw's work with Split Britches, all of which she wrote for her own voice in these collaborations with other performers and writers. These monologues are quintessential Shaw: boldly confrontational, politically astute, moving declarations of not just her complex characters but of Shaw's beliefs as a performer and as a person. In "Fat Lady," from *Upwardly Mobile Home,* one of the Split Britches trio's earliest productions, Shaw speaks as the formidable matriarch of the tiny family trying to win their way to a free recreational vehicle—and hence, a place to live—by competing in a bridge-sitting competition. The poignant monologue calls attention to the situation of looking and being looked at, to the body as spectacle, to the violence of the gaze, and to the material conditions of lesbian performance. Shaw teases spectators, drawing an analogy between herself and the fat lady at the circus who knows you're looking at her "being fat." "Do you want to see my legs?" she taunts. "That's expensive. I don't know if you have enough money to pay to see a lesbian grandmother's legs."

Evoking Shaw's expansive spirit, "Fat Lady" begins, "I am your mother. I am the Hudson River. I am the bridge. I am the traffic. I am the government here." Likewise, her monologue "The Big Lie," from *It's a Small House and We Lived in it Always* (1999, Split Britches in collaboration with Clod Ensemble), starts by declaring, "I cracked open an egg, / that vibrated the stove back and forth so hard / it created an earthquake that rattled the kitchen / till it shut off all the electricity below 14th Street / and set off every smoke alarm / in every apartment downtown." With a quotidian act like breaking an egg, Shaw establishes her connection with her building, her neighborhood, her city, and her country. Her actions have effects; electric wires spark and wake up Wall Street workers, who find themselves in an unusual emergency, their "Volvos rain[ing] down like meteor showers," desperate to secure their own insurance. "The Big Lie" rips the façade from American odes to freedom and democracy, revealing the stashes of privately held money that protect the rich and devastate the poor. "When the United States Constitution was written," Shaw reminds us, "95% of all Americans were either slaves or indentured servants." She brings history to life and challenges presumptions about how much progress we've since made to redress inequality.

In the song "Blue," also from *It's a Small House and We Lived in it Always,* Shaw adopts her own R & B idioms, once again digging beneath the surface—of the earth, the sea, the street—to grapple with the loss of love and the depths of despair. But finally, in the "Eight Questions" posed to Shaw by folks at the Walker Art Center when she performed there in 2005, Shaw finds the raw, resistant humor in the conditions that fuel her craft: being outside the norms of gender and class, sexuality and privilege.

Shaw says she loves to perform: "It's a meditative state. Nothing can touch you. You don't have any pain, you don't have any worries. You just have that hour of sheer meditation. And your body pumps that drug that gives you power and you can do anything. . . . I'm ready to die on those stages. . . . I think that would be awesome. Just to die in a performance. But I'm not planning to die." Shaw regrets that reviewers writing about her performances tend to be blinded by her gender play and forget that her work is built on craft. They tend to describe how handsome she is, she says, "and leave out that I'm a good performer. . . . I get marginalized as far as . . . my craft . . . which I have made from really nothing. . . . Me and Lois have developed an aesthetic from our desire. . . . But . . . we don't want to be reviewed on our sexuality."

Peggy Shaw might have received her education as a theater artist on the streets from drag queens, which means, she says, "You learn real fast. They wear heels, so you have to be tall. They're loud.

You have to be louder than them. They get in front of you. You have to get in front of them. You learn real fast how to be seen, how to be heard. It's a fast school." But now Shaw is teaching generations of her own students, passing down her lore, her tricks, her sleights of hand, and her brutal honesty about relationships that fail and the longing that doesn't leave. Shaw remains clear sighted about the constraints of her life, given the commitment she has maintained for so long to working her way, without compromise. She is saddled with the burden of pioneering gender performance; she teaches people how to see her work, as well as how to enjoy it and engage it and take it home with them to lives she hopes will be changed for the better by what they have experienced. "I want to be a certain kind of successful," she admits. Shaw relates that she once received "78 great reviews" but rues that she still performs "at a certain strata." "I get tired," she admits. "I just want to not have to work so hard." On the other hand, performance is not just what she does; it's who she is. "Most of these shows we can do 'til we're ninety," she says. "They're not based on any age. I hope I keep performing. I mean, I have to. That's what I do. I don't really know how to do anything else." Lucky for us.[11]

11. I'd like to thank LeAnn Fields, Peggy Shaw, Lois Weaver, Suzy Willson, Stacy Wolf, and the two anonymous readers, all of whose comments on earlier drafts of this essay were quite valuable to my writing. I appreciate their insights and their generosity. I would also like to thank Jaclyn Pryor, who joined me for the interviews of all the key players, and whose input was essential at the beginning of the process of editing this book.

On Being an Independent Solo Artist
(No Such Thing)

PEGGY SHAW

My name is Peggy Shaw.
I am a solo artist and, by virtue of that, a collaborator—
"I would be nothing without you."
Well, I would be something, but not all that I could be.
I write thousands of words, but I need others to edit them.
I move my body, but I need others to show me what it looks like
and light it in a space.
I sing and dance because I ask someone to make music and I have
my own company, so I can do anything I want.

There's another word for collaboration in the dictionary.
It means to be in cahoots with another country: a spy.
I could be defined in that way.
I travel from country to country
Slipping through borders to work.
I am a migrant worker.
With all due respect, I travel to where the work is.

You never know what's gonna happen in this process.

Because sometimes it works out great, and sometimes it's just plain
hard to figure out why you did it at all. As hard as I try, it's *because*
I believe in the artist in everyone, in the beauty of every person's
stories, that I have to eventually come back to believing in myself.

My work always starts with my own dreams and desires and tries to tell a truth, rather than having a message or a product. "I believe in new truths, not old lies." I feel privileged to be an artist, to be able to write what I call the creative truth. *Creative truth is when you take a basic impulse or a fact and try and make it poetic.*

I arrange my shows the way I paint a painting; this feels right, this seems like it goes there, this looks good. I like this color. I try not to question any of it. I just work on impulse.

And with an editor and a director, usually the same person.

And I work from love because in the end that is the question I ask myself; have I made this with love?

I make comedy by telling the truth—there is nothing funnier than the truth.

As a woman I never felt that I understood what was funny. I have devoted myself for forty years to making that discovery with an audience, whether it was learning from a regular theater or performance audience, or from women in prison, or people in college, or women in a domestic violence safe house, or creating a new show with eighteen Taiwanese women who didn't speak English.

What I really mean to say is that until I enter the room with people, whether it's a prison or a college (I often wish they were interchangeable, since I feel like it's a monetary situation), I have no idea what we will all come up with together as a collaboration. Pretty scary awesome way to live.

What you do see here is a solo show.

What you can't see here are all the details and all the weeks and hours that fill all the spaces in between with other people. In a way these images are not products but placeholders; these are moments that try and show you the thrill of making something that wasn't there before or the pain in trying to work in an honest way.

In my humble opinion, imagination, circumstance, and determination are what make everything happen.

In my art, I have been trying to describe the world that I have created while creating it. Never accepting the confines of the "normal" North American world, I make performance and theater, for those interested in hearing the poetry or point of view of a sixty-plus-year-old, second-generation Irish, working-class, grand-butch-mother.

I have been described as masculine. Actually I am a new kind of femininity. I am interested in testing masculine-feminine and butch-femme as markers. I want to go way beyond the boundaries of the girls' room and the boys' room. I see endless horizons and new ways of creating and defining ourselves on this difficult, greedy planet, which is weighted and distributed so heavily toward the white heterosexual masculine. It has seemed, at some points in my time here, that this planet wants to tip off its axis and spill all that bullshit into the black hole and start again. This particular political time is even darker than usual, with few visionaries to alter the course.

To me being an artist is paying very close attention to our surroundings and having the privilege of twisting the mirror in order to reflect new images back on the culture. I get up every day and do the best I can to create and teach new visions, not old ideas.

—Peggy Shaw
New York
September 2010

YOU'RE JUST LIKE MY FATHER

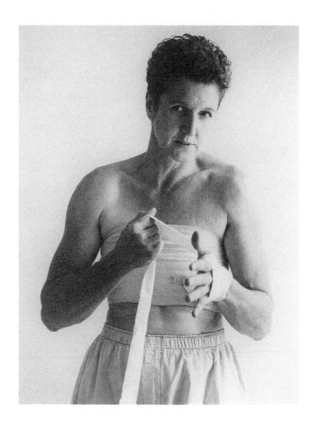

You're Just Like My Father
Written and performed by Peggy Shaw
Directed by Stacy Makishi and James Neale-Kennerly
Original lighting design by Rachel Shipp
Music and vocals by Laka Daisical
Additional vocals by Vick Ryder

You're Just Like My Father was developed at Dixon Place in New York and produced by the ICA in London and LaMama Theatre in New York.

Special thanks to Stormy Brandenberger, Stafford, Karena Rahall, Rose Sharp, Jill Lewis, Meryl Vladimer, Howard Thies, LaMama Etc., Rachel Shipp, Gay Sweatshop London, Lois Weaver, Hampshire College, WOW Café, Dixon Place, and New York Foundation for the Arts.

You're Just Like My Father was first published in *O Solo Homo: The New Queer Performance,* edited by Holly Hughes and David Román, Grove Press, 1998.

You're Just Like My Father

(Lights come up on Peggy sitting on a chair on a bare stage with bare breasts and boxer shorts, bare feet. She wraps her breasts with an Ace bandage and goes over to a suitcase on a table and opens it. The opening of the suitcase, like the opening of a music box, starts the song "You May Not Be an Angel." She gets another bandage from the suitcase and wraps it on top of the first bandage around her breasts. She takes another bandage from the suitcase and wraps a hand the way a boxer would, as the song finishes. When she is finished wrapping, she drops her head into her hands and growls like a wolf.)

The landlord wouldn't fix the toilet
'Cause he said there was nothing wrong with it.
She didn't know what she was planning on doing
She knew she had to do something.
You get no satisfaction calling in the authorities.
She watched the darkness in her window, waiting for some kind
Of release, but nothing came.
Her arms needed to strike out, to drive outside of her what was
Eating her up inside, but there was always such consequences
in wrecking a place to feel better.
She went over to the Kleenex box on the shelf, and started tearing
Up white pieces of Kleenex into tiny white squares,
Then she drew up the Kleenex in a little sack
and tied each one with a piece of string
This took her all afternoon
She waited until she knew that it would rain

and spread her tiny bundles all over
The big, beautiful, groomed, green lawn of his office.
It rained good and hard.
The next day the big, beautiful, groomed, green lawn
was dotted with
Hundreds of white specks of sugar stuck to the blades of grass,
There were no complaints to the management or to the police.
Only to the minister.
And the minister went to speak to the family, to her husband.
But since he was dead, he couldn't take the blame.
That is to say, my father couldn't take the blame.
'Cause this was my mother before they destroyed her.
My mother who was in love with me in the house.

(Runs her hands through her hair, making sound of a wolf.)

Hey!
I'm Eddie.
My father wouldn't call me Eddie, he called me Margaret.
Margaret means pearl.
I was his pearl of a girl.
But pearl didn't match my outfits.
This is my face. It's sharp like my father.
You look just like your father, my mother would say.
I look like my father when I'm in a good mood.
Most lesbians I know really like their fathers, me included.
My father was a Leo, he had a heart condition;
he had to count to ten before he hit us.
He gave me the same heart condition
simply because I knew him so well.
He had big hands. I have his big hands.
I like to touch things and people.
Once a shrink asked me where my desire comes from.
I said, "From my hands."
She told me to keep my hands to myself.

She didn't mean to say it.
It just came out and embarrassed her.
I guess shrinks aren't supposed to be so direct.
But I knew what she meant.
There were so many children in my family
that when we visited people's houses
we had to hold our hands behind our backs
for the whole visit
so we couldn't touch anything.
I had to control my hands all the time.
My Grandmother told me I would do great things with my hands;
I think she meant play the piano.
My father told me that his father knocked out Joe Louis
with his bare hands.

(Musical number: "This is a Man's World." During all the musical numbers, a microphone descends from the ceiling, as in a boxing ring. Music continues over.)

As hard
As I've tried
I can't get it up
Fully
On top
You know
Head
To toe
Missionary
Go tell it on the mountain
But mounting
Is something I've got trouble with
'Cause I can't
Get on top
Get hard
Butch on top

It's left over
From way back
When I was a boy
And all the girls
Wanted me to please
It's hard
To keep it up
My reputation
Easy for the young ones
But hard for me
But not hard enough.
If it only comes down
Or comes up
To coming
To keep it going
To keep it up
To strapping one on
To whacking me off
'Cause
Deep inside my love for you
Is a flash picture
It has to do with my arms
My fingers
My hands
These are the butch queer feminine parts
Of me
On the other hand
Either my left or my right
I'm told that I'm missing out on a dildo.
I can hardly look at the real ones
That look like real dicks
I can look at the dolphin ones
Dolphins don't have veins.
It's the veins.
That vanity in men.

I think Moby Dick was really a dolphin.
My father's dick looked like a dolphin
When I saw him
In the toilet.
Feminists made me hate dolphins, I mean dildos.
They tried to make me hate boxer shorts
Not that I want to put blame
On anyone for my
Lack of thrust
Except maybe the missionaries.
I don't want to be like my parents
In any way
Unless, of course,
I can't help it
You should never take your parents personally.

(Peggy goes to the center ring and counts down from ten, then dresses in the army uniform.)

My mother used to make me things from cardboard all taped together like houses. She used the cardboard from my father's Sunday shirts from the Chinese laundry. She caught me at the kitchen table at five years old, drawing a picture of a woman tied to a tree with her hands behind her and her breasts were naked, and I drew a woman kissing her breasts. My mother watched me closely from then on and made sure I didn't have girlfriends for too long or stay over at their houses. She said I'd go to hell if I didn't get married.

I liked other people's mothers. You know, around fifty, the ones who had to work in a store. They seemed like they could stand in one place without someone to protect them. But I wanted to sit with them in the kitchen for hours while they flirted with me. Their husbands seemed so old. And I was so full of desire. I would do things for them. And they never told me I was going to hell.

My mother hated my grandfather, and when he died, she didn't want to go to the funeral either, so we went to Brigham's in Cambridge and had a hot-fudge sundae. For years after that when I saw my mother I would take her for a hot-fudge sundae with marshmallow and nuts, I was her sundae lover. Once, we tried to go to a different ice-cream place. They didn't make it right, so they were wrong and she got mad. That's how she was about her family. Her family was right and the rest of the world was wrong.

(Peggy finishes dressing in her tie and hat. She salutes.)

My mother said, "You'll go to hell if you keep this up."
My mother said, "You'll die if you run in the street."
My mother said, "A bear will eat your child if you leave it
unattended on the back porch."
My mother said, "If you bowl on Sunday, you'll go to hell."
My mother said, "If you swear, you'll be like Catholics."
When I stand on my mother's shoulders I can see very far, sir!
I can see past my grandfather
and into the dripping water of the rain.

(Traveling music, such as in, for example, Pee Wee's Big Top.)

I always pack a gun.
That gives me the I'm okay, you're okay, look.
The one I use for borders.
Sometimes it works for me.
Once I went through a border with a drag queen,
who was dressed butch to pass as a man.
I was dressed femme to pass as a girl.
They pulled us over and wanted to see our suitcases.
He got my suitcase with the suits and ties and letters to girls.
I got his suitcases, with dresses and high heels and poems to boys.
They passed us through as normal.
But I didn't have my gun.
I didn't have my dildo.
Packing, I call it, in both cases.

I carry my gun, unlike my dildo.
I carry it just in case.
The gun that is.
I keep the dildo in my drawers
with my neatly folded white boxer shorts.
I don't use it. I'm not dangerous.
Knowing I'm safe makes me a trustworthy person.
You could even trust me with your wife if you wanted to.

(Peggy makes sugar bundles like those her mother let melt in the rain on the grass, wrapping mounds of sugar in tissue and tying them with string.)

Doctors say they aren't sure what ovaries do or what they're for, but I know that *en los ovaries* is my *luz de la vida. Luz de la vida* is not a type of gun, it's a joy of life. In Mexico, women carry the joy of life in their ovaries. Right now it's hard for you to find my ovaries because they're hidden by my fibroids, or barnacles, as I call them. When something is in the sea a long time, barnacles usually grow on it. But that's why it's harder and harder for me to find my joy in life. Well, not joy in my life, harder for me to find my ovaries. I only showed my barnacles to one woman in Seattle, and she looked in and said I had a beautiful cervix. Have you every had anyone tell you you had a beautiful cervix? Your body starts smiling from the inside and gets all perky and feeling good about itself. Whenever you have a chance, you should tell a woman you know that they have a beautiful cervix. As far as I know, cervixes aren't measured up to any standard of beauty, so you won't have anything to go by except your feelings. It doesn't matter if you believe anything I say or not.

It's just like my gun. I know it's there.
It's amazing that I still have sex.

(Traveling music.)

Or that I ever had sex.
When I was young
I thought everyone knew more than me about it.
All I knew was that when you grew up
you had to shave your pubic hair.
I knew that,
'cause I read page forty-nine
in my brother's book under his mattress.
I also thought that I would get pregnant wearing his dungarees.
Not so farfetched, really,
depending on how soon after he wore them.
I thought the other girls had secrets that they wouldn't tell me,
like there was something they wore in their underpants.
'Cause my friend, Joanne Brulee, who I loved more than anyone,
she let me kiss her sometimes.
Once in gym class I was helping her jump over the horse,
or the buck, as we called it,
I grabbed for her and my hand slipped between her legs.
I felt something hard, like a box in her underpants.
I can still feel it.
I try and think, still, what it was,
'cause it wasn't soft like a sanitary pad.
It felt more like the box they came in
in the vending machines in the girl's room.
I never found out 'cause she moved to Chicago and killed herself.

Maybe it was a gun between her legs.

(A short piece of circus music plays while Peggy slowly pulls a very long piece of paper out of her mouth.)

My mother said, "Every word you speak is forever in the air, it will never go away." She meant it as a threat to keep me from saying bad things, but I took it as a convenient sort of diary. A record that could be read any time. A record with its needle stuck in a groove, playing the same song over and over again. Unforgiving. It's only now that I realize that these words can be used against me. Or would come back to haunt me.

(Peggy lays the sugar bundles she's made across the front of the stage, creating a line of them between herself and the audience.)

I would have joined the army in the early sixties if *Life* magazine hadn't published their latest test for detection for homosexuals in the army. They made you look through these binocular-type glasses to watch slides of naked women, and if your eyes dilated when you saw a naked body of the same sex, then you were kicked out of the army in disgrace. I remember when I read it, my grandfather was dozing off in his favorite chair in the afternoon, after complaining about modern things, how they make too much noise and the air used to be clean, and that made him cry, only his tears were because he married the wrong woman. He was showing my grandmother Cicely an engagement ring he had bought for another woman and she thought it was for her and she accepted the marriage proposal and he was too embarrassed to explain the truth, so he married her and they were together fifty-five years.

I caught on to my legacy.
I caught on to the game in time.
There was life before I knew about the ring,
and my life after the ring.
My mother brought me up to be polite
so I try not to ask women to marry me unless I mean it.

(Shadow-boxing.)

My mother used to tell me that there's a line in your head that if you cross over too far, you go crazy. There's also the line that if you think backwards too far, you have no room for the new stuff. My mother said that women weaken the legs.

(Peggy removes the army uniform, folding it carefully and putting it in her suitcase. She puts on a lounge robe instead.)

My mother said quotation marks change the meaning of things; make them more important, just like the meaning of the written word. They frame meaning, like the name that tries to frame being. It's a simple out, naming me reminds you of your father, as if there are only two choices in life, mother and father. But I'll take that on if that's your only way of describing it. It's a simple out, merely an imitation of a man we all know. Guilt by association. Not very fatherly. Be careful of the company you keep because they are witnesses and they might just quote you someday.

What are you thinking?
Right then?
Yes.
I don't remember.
Were you thinking about her?
No, I . . . I was thinking about how much work I have to do.
I know you weren't thinking about work,
it's not the same look . . . I know what you're thinking.
You think you know what I'm thinking,
if you knew, you wouldn't ask.
Do you want her more than me?
No.
Yes, you do. How could you not? It's so new . . .
It's just . . . different.
I like seeing you together. I like the way you look at her.
It brings me back.
You like her 'cause that's how I used to be.
Don't be silly, you're still like that.
What if you fall in love with her?
You're more in love with her than I am.
Maybe. But you and I are different.

I know.
So you'll probably fall in love with her
and she'll break your heart.
And I'll have to live with it.
You're very casual.
I'm not afraid of losing you. I'll always love you.
What are you thinking?
The same thing you are.
Stop.
It makes me feel close to you without really talking.
I could get up right now and leave you right here with yourself.
Don't touch me.
You have a beautiful body.
You take up space before I can even think about where I'm going.
Before I can even decide where to go next,
you've moved there already.
We're different.
I guess that was our attraction.
Come here.
No.
What do you mean, was our attraction, it still is.
We're just standing too close.
Move away, give me some room.
Okay.
Don't leave me!
You're a fool. You were a fool for me.
You're a fool for anyone who falls in love with you.
I'm a fool but I'm smart, I fell in love with you.
Make me understand.
I need a written contract that you desire me and I need it renewed
every day, signed by a witness. Witnessed by you know who.
So is that the attraction? The witness?
It helps me see my love, it helps me feel my truth.
Her truth.

Truth through her.
What about her?
What about her?
She's just a witness?
No she's very special. A very sensitive, smart, loving . . .
Trusting
Trusting
We've been here before
Not like this. This suspension, this heightening feeling, this
inability to go too deep 'cause
you're watching me. It makes it unbearable.
Lovely.
How can I watch you if you're so close?
I'll move.
Don't leave me!
I want to witness you, I want a lover, rather, I want another lover.
You've got it!
Just like that?
You convinced me it could only add up
to an already sexy situation.
Can I get a witness?

(Spit.)

My mother told me that black pepper caused brain damage.
She told me that she thought black people
were born in the night.
She told me I couldn't have Coca-Cola until I was sixteen, and
When I had one at a lunch counter, she said Catholics
Made me do it.

(Spit.)

She told me she loved the name Peggy, it was a beautiful name.
The first, sweetest thing any girl ever told me was that she

was at a drive-in movie with her boyfriend Paul
and while they were making out she had whispered my
name by mistake, and Paul drove her right home
and threw up all over her lawn. It filled me with fear and
power at the same time.
The fear came from being caught for the pervert that I was.
The power came from the effect it had on the lawn.
I always associate wrecking lawns with power.

(Spit.)

Every time someone hurts me, I want to become famous
and buy a 1962 Corvette and get all dressed up
with a beautiful woman next to me,
and drive past them on the street,
just so they can catch a glimpse of me
and how happy and successful I am.
I got that from Jimmy Cagney.

(Rock and roll music in the style of The Duals' "Stick Shift.")

I associate everything with cars, except my sexuality, that I attribute to my hands. The only thing I liked about *Desert Hearts* was
when she went backwards really fast in her truck.

(Rock and roll music continues under monologue.)

I got really excited when I realized that my sexuality was also in my
lips. I got that from Elvis Presley. He taught me to pay attention to
my lips. I would try to sneer like him when flirting with girls, and
that's when I developed the habit of licking my lips, to keep them
moist and desirable. I felt like most people were staring at my lips
at a time when most girls thought people were staring at their
breasts. Sometimes I had to cover my lips with my hands because
they felt vulnerable and naked, and dangerous and out of control.

I used to pretend that my hand, that soft part between the index finger and the thumb was Marie Manjouritis's lips. And I would kiss that part of my hand and put my tongue through the opening. I would feel embarrassed when I saw her because I thought that she would remember how passionate my kiss was and tell someone and put me in sex jail.

The man I am today still thinks all desire starts at the mouth. It comes from right inside the lip, the inside part of the lips that are always moist.

(Music fades.)

The only part of getting old that I worry about is that my lips will dry up and be hard and wrinkly, and that thought's enough to break me into a sweat in the middle of the day, let alone the middle of the night.

Meanwhile, my mother was watching and flirting with me.

(Peggy puts her hands over her face and makes the sound of the wolf, as she did at the beginning. She puts a blood pressure cuff on her arm.)

I went into the subway at West Fourth Street in the summer, and came out in Brooklyn in the fall. That's how fast time is moving, moving along with my blood. My blood is trying to tell me something, clotting up and trying to torture me so it can get out of me, moving through me in blood clots of magnitude. My blood is a volcano. I met the goddess Pele at the volcano. I offered my body as a sacrifice to Pele, a butch girl sacrifice. Pele likes butches and prefers eating them to almost anyone else. Nice to have a goddess who prefers you. Like Pele, I have high blood pressure. My acupuncturist, who thinks he's Tom Jones, is trying to lower my fire so I won't burn myself up. But I'm afraid that the combination of that and menopause will make me a boring person. What would a volcano be without her lava? Without her blood?

When I see blood, I want to eat it, chew it up good, or chop it up with onions for chopped liver, put an egg over it and have steak tartare, salt and pepper and some Worcestershire sauce, put it in a blender and add ice for a nice summer drink, a cranberry blood clot or a bloody Mary, but Mary's not here to hold back my hands. I'm down in Pele, reaching for her womb, keep my hands to myself. Keep these big, old, cow-milking, queer hands to myself. Let them hang at my side or behind my back, or slip into my own pants and stay there. Big old hands that want to get sucked into you, sliding uncontrollably up into you, too big to get in, like a newborn baby, ready for the womb, but not the world.

(Peggy does her imitation of a "femme" walk to the suitcase. She takes off the lounge robe, folding it away in the suitcase, and begins to dress in a suit.)

My mother used to watch me getting dressed.
I used to let myself take forever getting dressed.
My mother watched me.
She loved me, my mother.
She recognized me.
"You look just like your father," she said.
I put on a starched shirt
And I was my father.
I loved how my father's few Sunday shirts
Looked and smelled when they came back
From the Chinese laundry,
And had a piece of cardboard inside
To keep them rectangular and stiff.
Very stiff and starched.
They had peach-colored bands around them
Keeping all the long sleeves
And tail tucked in.
When he unfolded his white shirt Sunday morning
It kept its rectangular shapes
All over the shirts and the cuffs.

And the cuffs were huge and flat and spreading
Out at the bottom of the sleeve
'Cause it hadn't been folded for cuff links.
I wanted to have a starched white shirt like his,
Keeping it safe all week,
Knowing it's in a drawer piled on top of other shirts
And the white folded boxer shorts.
Men's underwear folds so neatly and square.
Women's underwear doesn't have a real logic to it.
And my father had this great gesture after he shaved
Of patting his cheeks with cologne
And running his hands all around his face.
When I touched my own face like that, in a kind of
Rough way, my mother would say,
"Don't touch your face like that, you'll wreck your skin."
But she liked my father's leathery skin
And the way he was pulling up his chin
the whole church service, away from the starched shirt collar.
My mother always held his hand in church,
And seemed fragile, like she would break
If my father's white shirt wasn't there
Keeping the world from caving her in.
Just the idea of the world could cave in my mother.
That's why I chose to be a boy.
So I could wear starched shirts
To keep the ugly world away from girls,
And so girls could hold my hand
And rest their head on my shoulder
My clean white shoulder, stiff with pleasure.

(Sings crooner song in the style of Albert Hammond's "To All the Girls I've Loved Before" in the audience.)

When I was twenty-one, I died because of love in a heat wave.
I slept with a woman for the first time and went
Into a coma from spinal meningitis that lasted two weeks.

At twenty-one, I already died for love, so I know how it feels.
It sort of clanks
Like empty glass bottles on a tray
Banging into each other
And I can't do anything about it.
I can't even reach the place
the clanking is coming from.
It's like a coma,
A kind of chosen place
A definitive space
Nearby
Where I go for a while
Until I can recover enough to function.
Love's an oral thing
Trying to put your whole body into my mouth,
At least into my vision.
I want to capture you,
For just a moment.
Looking out the window sometimes works
Conjuring up your voice
Close to my ear
Remembering what it is I love so much about you.
Have you ever had a song caught in your head?
It's like the needle's stuck in a groove and the song plays
Over and over.
While I was floating in my coma
I heard Fats Domino singing, "I wanna be a wheel . . ."
And then applause and then repeat again, "I wanna be . . ."
And then applause.
This went on for three days and three nights.
And I begged the nurse to stop that song,
But there wasn't any music playing.
I wanted it to stop but that needle was unforgiving,
Like the heat wave,
Unforgiving, like my daily spinal tap
I knew it was coming

By the clanking sound
Of empty bottles
On a tray, rattling down the hall.
They'd stick an empty needle into my spine
And that needle was unforgiving, like the heat wave,
Unforgiving, like my mother.

My mother used to tell me that if you take something beautiful and repeat it many times, it becomes more beautiful.

My mother held my hand for two weeks and when the heat wave felt forgiving, she pulled the plug from the fan and the music stopped.

"Do you know you look just like your father? You remind me of him. Do you want a pair of his cuff links? I know where they are. How about a tie? I have one of his summer ties. Oh, how you remind me of him when he was a young farmer, he had those muscles in his forearms that stuck out from milking cows."

And she remembered him. I dressed my mother's memories. "But don't let your sisters see you, you know how they copy you, I don't want them dressing like that, and I worry about you, that you're going to hell because of the way you dress, eternal hell to burn with the devil. And I don't want you bringing your sisters with you."

(A sentimental song plays like "I'm Confessing that I Love You.")

I shined my shoes while they were on, and my mother smiled. "You look just like your father," she said. I think she wanted me to kiss her hand. I put on my hat to leave and the spell was broken. She forgot who I was, she forgot I was her Sunday lover, and she said I would burn in hell. I let myself take forever getting dressed. My mother loved me. She recognized me.

(Peggy salutes and leaves with the suitcase. The song continues through the curtain call.)

Fat Lady

I am your mother. I am the Hudson River. I am the bridge, I am the traffic. I am the government here.

I am the police. That makes me invisible. I am your hope. I am the bluest skies you have ever seen and water and food. I am big arms that hold you. I love you when you are unhappy, I love you the way you are. I laugh, I scream, I have to laugh.

Once when I was young, I went to a fair and saw a sign to see a fat lady for twenty-five cents. I gave the booth my money and walked into the tent to see my fat lady. It was a big tent. I was alone. There was a fat lady sitting on a couch with her legs propped up on two stools, and her arms supported by pillows. She was alone. I looked at her, she looked at me. She knew I had come to see her being fat! I ran out of the tent exhausted. I knew her, she was me. We were looking at each other. But I was tricked. The colors, the music, the lights, promised me entertainment, but gave me much more than that. I was right there at one with myself, me and that fat lady. I wish I was still there sometimes. I still remember the daylight seeping through the pinholes in the tent. I remember her fat was there overpowering me but I couldn't look at her. I love that fat lady!

(Sings "I'm gonna be a wheel one day . . .")

From *Upwardly Mobile Home* by Peggy Shaw, Lois Weaver, and Deb Margolin, 1984.

You have paid to see me. You won't get your money back. Your money does not pay me for my work. I work always.

What circle do you move in? Do you have a bed to sleep in? And food? And a toilet? Do your friends? Do you have a need to share your life with others? Tell stories? Do you get paid for your stories? Do you get paid what you are worth for your work? Am I worth the price you paid for your ticket to see this play today?

Do you want more room to watch me in? A bigger theater? More comfortable seats? Are you willing to pay for that? Or do you want to pay for a more comfortable show? I am a grandmother, a good grandmother. Are you willing to pay to see a good lesbian grandmother?

My legs feel long and keep getting in my way. Do you want to see my legs? That's expensive. I don't know if you have enough money to pay to see a lesbian grandmother's legs.

I wear a suit for every time I see a fat lady. I wear a tie for every time I cry. If I sell my suit and tie, I have money to buy food. If I lose my suit and tie, I have my memories. When I am rich, I will buy my mother a house and a car and a family.

MENOPAUSAL GENTLEMAN

Menopausal Gentleman
Written by Peggy Shaw, 1997
In collaboration with and directed by Rebecca Taichman
Choreography by Stormy Brandenberger
Music, sound effects, and arrangements by Vivian Stoll
Suit design by Mirena Rada

This show is dedicated to James Neale-Kennerley.

Menopausal Gentleman was commissioned and first presented in New York City by Dixon Place, with funds from the Joyce Mertz-Gilmore Foundation and the Heathcote Art Foundation, and was subsequently produced off Broadway at the Ohio Theatre in a co-production with the Ohio Theatre and Ellie Covan.

Menopausal Gentleman

(Pre-show music in the style of Barry White. Peggy Shaw appears in a single column of front white light from up high with a blue back light, suggestive of street corner or film noir movie style. She is dressed in high drag: perfectly fitted wide-shouldered men's double-breasted pin-striped suit with breasts strapped down for the full "passing" effect; fresh, short "men's" haircut with pomade; white starched shirt, 1940's red pattern tie with tie clip, white handkerchief folded perfectly in breast pocket, high-shined dark red wing-tipped shoes.)

I was walking and wrapped myself around a tree downtown. The tree smashed into my chest and took my breath away. Before I fell, before I slowed down by slamming into a tree, I appeared perfectly normal.

There are better ways to slow down.

Let me try and describe it to you . . . what it all looks like, and how it all takes place inside my body, from the dusk to the dawn of the nighttime in my body.

I'm trying to pass as a person when there is a beast inside me, a beast on fire who waits in the shadows of the night. Pacing and sweating and turning, a beast in captivity in my body, moving about, the same patterns over and over, wearing out grooves in my floor.

(Takes out handkerchief and wipes her brow coolly, then returns handkerchief neatly to pocket.)

Sweat is big, lots of sweat, fanning myself with a big fan I keep by my bed. A fan with a painting of the woods on it that I use to hide my wet face . . . I also have a room-divider: one side is the sea, one side is the woods. I keep fresh handkerchiefs by my bed. I wash them every day and iron them and neatly fold them.
I have a ceiling fan painted amber, the fan is in front of the night light so there's an effect of striped lighting moving through the fan, almost like a train moving through my night giving me the feeling that I'm getting somewhere. It's 4 a.m., they call it the hour of the wolf, the dangerous time. It's not night and it's not morning. Tiger Time. I never go out at that hour 'cause I could slip right through and disappear forever.

I can't sleep.
I'm all wet.

I wonder if my heart ever skips a beat.
Do you worry about it? I do.
I lie on my heart side and I can feel it
beating pounding into the bed.
Zip me up. Mop me.
On the street I'm on the outside.
Like a furnace on the inside,
sweating in the cold.
My shirt is wringing wet.
My back is dripping all the way to the waist.
Like an outline. Of sweat. Licking my hand.

I wonder what it sounds like. When it skips a beat.
huh
I don't remember hearing sounds so loud before.
Driving me crazy. Sounds in the wall like car engines
or a boiler room or air conditioning.
If there was a car engine within a mile of here I would hear it.
It must have been so quiet before they invented cars.

Just the sound of the dinosaurs and dripping water on rocks,
like sweat.
yeah
I get scared when I hear a heart beating in my ear.
yeah
like when I have my head on your chest.
oh
I hear your heart beating like a big machine.
huh
I hear my own heart beating in my neck
really loud inside my body
Like a big machine, that runs the world.
Every night when I do go to sleep
my bed drops down into the engine room that runs my night.
Like light coming out of the inside of my trailer.

My heart beats fast in my neck and in my jaw,
like a fist clenching and unclenching.
I throw off the covers and look for water.
Beads of sweat are starting to form at the edges of my hair again
like bugs
and I'm sweating, the sweat forcing me to sleep alone.
My family says I exhaust them when I visit
'cause I question everything,
I find them exhausting 'cause they accept things as they are.
The inside of my body seems so fragile.
I was always afraid to put my fingers inside me.
Funny how women's sex is on the inside,
men's is on the outside.
That's just the way it goes.
This body is inside this suit.
This suit will give you an idea of what I feel like.
Inside I'm all strapped down
'cause you can't have a great suit like this
and have bumps on the outside.

I'm not afraid of what's inside me!
I don't have to do anything
when I feel *it* inside me. The Tiger.
My tiger looks up in the night
and sees the blue blue sky vibrating through
the green green leaves
and doesn't HAVE to fuck it
own it
grab it
wish it
take it
change it
hold it
touch it
paint it
or please it . . . but it would be fun to try.

Like Tina Turner, I'm gonna start real slow
and then I'm gonna get rough.
Touch you on the cheek
brush my hand lightly on your lips,
kiss your shoulder
after I pull your sweater down
and pin you against the wall
making sure you feel the cold wall against
your shoulders as I kiss them.
Go down on my knees.

(Goes down on knees.)

Making sure I still have a firm hold on you.
Rip off your pants with my teeth.
GRRRRRRRR. That's the Tiger part!
Lift you up high and hold you there
so you can take the time to smell the rain.

Start talking to you real low like Barry White . . .
In the dark!

(A song plays, in the style of Nina Simone singing "In the Dark," as the lights fade to black. As the song plays, Peggy hides flashlights in her sleeves and her pant legs, which, when she turns them on, light up only her hands and her feet on the otherwise dark stage. She dances, while the light makes her limbs seem disembodied. The song continues until it ends, while Peggy dances and speaks in the dark.)

Just the beat of my poor heart
skips a beat in the dark.
I wonder if my heart ever skips a beat.
Do you worry about it? I do.
Do you worry about me
when you see me break into a sweat on the subway?
I travel for hours and hours in a situation that should terrify me.
I went out of the house
in a pink white and blue
striped cotton summer starched shirt
and I was sweating.
Everyone on the train was wearing gloves and scarves
and black winter coats.

(Peggy takes the flashlights out of her sleeves, leaving the two in her pant legs.)

Everyone is staring at me
'cause I'm sweating so much in the cold car.
They think I'm a criminal.
A guy in the middle of winter in summer clothes
breaking into a cold sweat.
I wouldn't mind but my private summer
messes up my starched shirts.

I take a 15½ neck in a shirt
but I like them bigger
'cause I can't stand anything tight or I sweat around my neck
and I feel like I'm going to choke.
I could choke in a second.
I could choke to death.
Well, choke until I die.

My father had five sisters: Catherine, Helen, Alice, Ruth, and
Marion. The first letter from each of their names spells CHARM,
so they were called the CHARM Sisters. Each one choked to death.
Well, they coughed for years before they finally choked till they
died. I'm not gonna choke to death. I'm not gonna die like
Tennessee Williams, the way he supposedly choked on a bottle
cap, and the way they tried to make me believe Mama Cass
choked to death in bed on a chicken sandwich.

It's hard to be a gentleman in menopause.

I just hope they don't put me away before this is all over,
or give me shock treatments.
They tried to shock my mother out of her change.
If I change and they put me away will you come and get me?
Menopause is all it's made up to be.
I'm insane, I don't sleep,
If I was president I'd blow up the world,
and then the next day I'd say,
I really shouldn't have blown up the world like that.
The reason I like the word gentleman is how refined
and detailed and consistent it is.
The opposite of how I feel.
I'm erratic on the inside and I try to be consistent on the outside,
so that I appear perfectly normal.
Mixed with the sweat.
I have nice breasts for a boy.
You describe me as a 54-year-old woman

who passes as a 35-year-old man
who likes the ladies.
A woman passing as a man looks like a younger man,
a man passing as a woman
looks like an older woman.
That's just the way it goes.
I keep young by passing, you see.
I sacrifice being a woman for youth. It's a trade-off.

(Music starts to a song in the style of Louis Armstrong's "Brand New Suit."
Peggy sings the words live and dances as if it's a memory from the 1930s—
Jimmy Durante/Fred Astaire combo. She talks over the end of the music.)

My friend in San Francisco thinks I'm her father,
she called me and said can she put her trailer on my land.
I said of course.
She says to me, Thanks, Dad.
I say, You're welcome, Son.
It is a beautiful moment.

(Music ends.)

Being a . . . *(Fixes tie.)*
Being a gentleman *(Hands on hips spreading suit jacket.)*
Being a gentleman is very . . . *(Hands on crotch.)*
Being a gentleman is very important to me.
In the daytime I'm a fairy tale tiger passing as a gentleman
A tiger looking swell
I got five planets in ego—Leo!
Big one tiger with five planets in lion.
I love being a tiger.
I thought I was a lion
but every time I try and say lion
it turns my tongue to a T instead
and comes out tion, tigron, tigger, tiger, big-one tiger,
tion, tigron, tigger, tiger,

grrrrrrr, growler, a Siberian big-one tiger!
and my tongue sticking out of my Siberian tiger teeth
'cause I'm smelling sound with a smelling sense
on the top of my nostrils.
Aloha from One-Big tiger.
Grrrrr it's hard to growl like a tiger.
Gotta get the sound coming from my chest,
I have to concentrate to keep my voice low,
to match my suit.
Otherwise when I open my mouth to speak
it's like what happened when movies went from silents to talkies,
and actors lost their jobs
'cause their voices didn't match their bodies.
You gotta . . . *(Hands on tie.)*
You gotta spend . . . *(Hands on hips, spreading suit jacket.)*
You gotta spend a lot . . . *(Hands on crotch.)*
You gotta spend a lot of time being a gentleman.
I'm the hardest-working gentleman in show business.
Being a gentleman means my shoes are shining.
Shoes are one of the elements of gentlemanness.
And cufflinks.
And whistling. *(Wolf whistle.)* Dig that crazy chick!

(Sounds of birds, animals, etc., especially growling of a tiger. "I'm a Man" music starts—like a talking blues with tiger sound effects done in "male" gestures.)

When I was a little girl
to set things right
I made a little adjustment
in the middle of the night

Now I'm a Man
aged like wine
I could make love to you baby
in an hour's time

'Cause I'm a Man
Spelled M*A*N Man
oh oh oh oh

I don't lose my cool
'cause I use my mind
so many women
so little time

'Cause I'm a man
Spelled M*A*N Man
oh oh oh oh

Now I'm older
Youth I don't miss
My change has come
Has come to this

I'm a man
Spelled M*A*N Man

(Over the music and growling.)

Menopause is seeing a pigeon
flying above the traffic on St. Marks Place and Second Avenue
with a whole slice of pizza in its mouth!

*(Peggy moves behind the bench upstage, growling and lip-synching the
tiger's noise. The song ends suddenly.)*

I worry because to me menopause is all of my characteristics
blown up a million times,
and all my life I have been in agony
over missing.
Could I live if I missed a million times more?

I miss you.
There are no curves on me and no flies.
I make sure of that,
and I never kiss on the street,
just can't do it.
It's hot in here, isn't it?

(Wipes face with handkerchief.)

Turn the heat down, I'm going down
The temperature is down
downtown
sweating in the cold night.
I never sleep anymore.
When I start feeling tired at night
I'm real careful
to move very slowly toward the bed
so I won't wake myself up.
I don't even risk brushing my teeth.
I pick up the sheet and slowly slip under it
and lie down.

(The lights dim, so that the stage atmosphere resembles the light and feeling of 4 a.m. Peggy slowly lies down on the beach, starting in an impossibly tense posture.)

I start at my toes and I say, okay toes,
you just relax and take it easy,
calm, calm,
that's it,
time to go to sleep,
yes, okay ankles and legs,
now you join in the calm
and stop jumping and stay still, that's it

(Body starts to relax as each part is described.)

The knees a little relaxed, untense yourself knees,
just feel the ocean rhythm coming in and going out,
yes, thighs I want you to join the rest of the leg and foot
and set a good example for my belly and my hips,
feel the blood
moving up from the feet—
yes, that's it, hips, just relax, good hips,
good belly, good legs, good feet, good uterus,
okay stomach,
I know I ate too late
but follow the example,
stop gurgling and turning over,
set a good example for the rest of the body
like the arms and the hands,
lay quietly on the bed, hands,
good hands,
almost asleep,
yes,
all you fingers just relax,
feel the ocean rhythm coming in and going out—
now my chest and my heart,
I'm slowing my breathing to rest my big enlarged heart,
so big it sticks up when I lie down
but I'm not going to think of my heart now
'cause I'm almost there,
okay throat,
that's a hard one, my throat,
everything is jammed up in my throat,
let it go,
that's it, good throat,
yes, eyes,
just picture the sea the waves rolling in and out
lapping on the shore, keep gently closed

(Her whole body is relaxed, except the head. Long pause.)

Okay brain! Hello brain, that's it,
we're almost all asleep,
hello brain,
yes, sleep like everyone else,
come on brain,
you know how important it is to be still and peaceful,
well you can try brain, can't you?
I know I don't have any health insurance,
it's okay, I'm not gonna get sick.
Just try a little bit, brain,
come on you can do it,
I know I wasn't a good mother,
it was the 70s, no one was a good mother in the 70s,
well you're not even trying,
what do you mean you're worried about October,
it's July! *Can't you just think of the ocean rhythm coming in
and going out!*
okay brain, I give up . . .
EVERYBODY UP!!

*(Jumps up to a standing position while smacking the different parts of her
body awake with her hands.)*

I throw off the covers and I'm up for another five hours.

(Standing still with eyes looking left.)

The red light on the stereo is keeping me awake

(Standing still with eyes looking right.)

and that VCR clock is flashing 12 o'clock—12 o'clock—12 o'clock.
I jump up and cover it with a towel.

Even a sliver of light under the door from the hallway
keeps me up.

I console myself by licking my hands, my paws, my menopause.
I have a tiger in my tank.
I can't keep my paws off you.
Grrrrrr
After spending the day with you, I gasp when I look in the mirror.
My face is as rusty as a dug-up piece of metal.
Dangerous.
Cut my hand on my face if I'm not careful.
Scratch the skin off my fingers.
I just move my head and it cuts the air.
I'm scared that when the snow melts,
I'll find all those things I forgot to put away.
Or all those things I lost,
or I didn't know I had before it snowed.
My mother dreamt a tiger was chasing her for 35 years.
She had the same dream over and over again every night.
Just before it got her, she'd wake up,
throw off the covers and pray.
Get out of my dreams.
I'm nervous. It's okay, some of my best friends are nervous.
I'm nervous 'cause I'm not ready for the change.
Bad dreams
too many covers
wrinkles
brittle bones
over the hill
downhill
no sleep
sweat
What should I do? This isn't funny.
Don't panic. Grrrr
I feel these original sins burning into me like I'm never safe.

There I am at 4 a.m.
with giant monsters spelling out my life
in large slimy letters above my body,
just far enough above it to heat it up.
To make my skin bead in sweat
starting just under my hair
above my forehead,
on the back of my neck,
on my chest
and behind my knees.
Don't panic. Grrrr

I was born this way.
I was born butch.
I didn't learn it at theater school!
I'm so queer I don't even have to talk about it, it speaks for itself.
It's not funny.
An older woman being a gentleman is not funny.
Don't panic.
Menopause is not funny.
Well, maybe in the daytime, in the light. . . .
I fall to pieces in the night.
I'm just thousands of parts of other people mashed into one body.
I am not an original person.
I take all these pieces,
snatch them off the floor where they land
before they get swept under the bed by the light,
and I manufacture myself.
When I'm saying I fall to pieces,
I'm saying Marlon Brando was not there for me.
James Dean failed to come through,
where was Susan Hayward when I needed her,
and Rita Hayworth was nowhere to be found.
I fall to pieces at the drop of a hat.

(Instrumental music for a song in the style of "My Way" comes on.)

Just pick the piece you want
and when I pull myself back together again
with the morning light,
I'll think of you.
I'll think of you and who you want me to be.

*(Peggy moves into the audience, speaking the song as a poem. When the
spoken song ends, the chords of the music continue under her monologue,
which she continues to address to the audience.)*

I know now I didn't eat enough tofu.
You're supposed to start really young.
You should start right away.
In Japan they don't even have a word for hot flashes.
I don't know if I can live the rest of my life like this.
Everything is catching up to me.
That feeling I had in 1977 that I never dealt with in Amsterdam.
I have gotten to the end of my blood.
Where has it all gone to?
What excuse do I have for my moods or tears
or not being able to fall asleep
now that I can't count on my blood anymore for an excuse?

(Peggy leaves the audience and returns to the stage.)

They say women have a certain amount of eggs
to use up in a lifetime. I DID IT!
My companions of forty years (the blood) have left me.
Like the boarded up Polish store on Ninth Street
that used to have fresh eggs on Thursdays.
The good old days.
When I had eggs!
I'm a grandmother gentleman now,
and have a three-year-old grand-companion-son.
I think we get along so well
'cause we're both going through a lot of the same things:

we're experimenting with saying no.
He understands me.
We go for long walks together on the edge.
I took him one Sunday to the Museum of Natural History.
As good a place as any to start teaching him
not to believe everything he reads—
as if they can tell that a rock is three million years old.
They make it all up!
I couldn't read the inscriptions to him in good conscience,
so I made up my own stories
about how the dinosaurs exist now,
only on a separate plane,
and if you drink too much alcohol
or take bad drugs
the electric shield around your body breaks down
and that's when you can see how close the dinosaurs are to us.
Then I let him run really far and fast
'cause that is the best thing about the museum of Natural History,
he can break into a run on a shiny marble floor.
I figure that's enough to learn for one day.
As he was leaving
I also told him not to try to make an oil painting in Florence,
or a play in London
'cause they're full of them already.

Maybe parents stay too long with their children.
Maybe you're not supposed to spend so many years together.
It's like being in love.
They say it takes as long to get over someone
as how long you were with them.
Like grieving,
not understanding why the sun still comes up anymore.
Then one morning
you wake up
and realize you haven't thought about that person
and you've already had your coffee.

I remember when I hadn't thought of my mother for a whole day.
It made me so sad.
When I realized it,
I wept and wept
and was scared that I was capable of forgetting her.

(Fake Barry White mood music in background, words spoken in the style of Barry White.)

I ran out of luster in my hair a few years ago.
The sun is merciless when you're in your fifties.
You do love me in the daylight, don't you?
In the amber light? In the night light
My mother told me there's nothing in the dark
that's not in the light.
I can hear you breathing but I can't see you.
What did you say?
There's a word for me.
Apart from the one that springs to your lips.
I have a short memory.
You're not the first one disappointed
that I don't act the way I look.

(Music ends.)

It's okay that someone who loves you doesn't necessarily feed you organic food or keep you off antibiotics. Just that you know you're loved, so that when you're walking on a snow-covered hill with the moon lighting up the night like daylight and the shadows are purple grey and there's no one around for miles, that you feel loved, and you know that someone kissed the moon before it got to you.

night flashes
hot night
sweaty clothes

insanity
insomnia
in the dark
menopause
the menopause blues
calcium, calcium, *calcium is big.*

My head bone connected to my neck bone
My neck bone connected to my shoulder bone
My shoulder bone connected to my back bone
My back bone connected to my hip bone
My hip bone connected to my thigh bone
My thigh bone connected to my knee bone
My knee bone connected to my ankle bone
My ankle bone connected to my foot bone
Now hear the words of the lord
Dem bones dem bones dem   dry bones
Dem bones dem bones dem   dry bones
Dem bones dem bones dem   dry bones
Now hear the words of the Lord

(A light that looks both spooky and celestial shines down on Peggy from directly above, which signals her move into the next musical number, a wild, scary lip-sync to a song in the style of Screamin' Jay Hawkins's "I Put a Spell on You." Peggy does a macabre dance that makes it seem like the song is controlling her body. When it ends, her suit jacket is on backwards, making it look as though her arms are sticking out the back of her coat.)

My head is leaking like a can of outdated film.
Light is seeping through cracks in my brain
and exposing it, wiping out all the millions of images
stored in there like a movie warehouse.
When I look at a sunset or a movie screen,
I am disrupted by big floaty things in my eyes.
I used to pretend they were scratches on my glasses.
I know now it's the breakdown of light in my brain.

Like night is falling under water.
I'm made out of material that's a little worse for wear.

They say a lot of women get like men in menopause
'cause they grow a beard and get dried out.
I guess that's their definition of man.
A hairy, dried-up woman.
Want some advice?
I'll give you some advice,
want it?
Okay, here goes,
picture yourself on your death bed
thinking about your life
all of a sudden you remember her, how beautiful she was
and you say to yourself,
while slapping your forehead with the palm of your hand,
"I shoulda fucked her!"

(Peggy puts her hand to her forehead and the lights change. The mood slows
way down, while music plays. She moves to the bench and drains a bottle of
water she finds below it. Then she sits on the bench and slowly, calmly
removes the flashlights from her ankles. A song in the style of Toni Childs's
"Where's the Ocean" plays as an instrumental in the background. Peggy
continues her monologue over this music.)

I go for rides in my car at 4 a.m. to cool down.
I open all the windows to air myself out.
I keep them all open while I drive at 55
just to feel all that cold at my neck and face,
to feel the night air moving on my skin
giving me the feeling that I'm getting somewhere.
I asked you if you would spend the night with me
and you made me promise not to go to sleep
or turn off the light
and that was easy for me. I stayed up all night thinking
and counting your breaths.

I was surprised that my longing didn't wake you
'cause it felt like a big boat tied to a dock
straining at the ropes
making that tough noise ropes make
when they're squeezed hard against wood.
Lying next to you
I could see there were tiny holes in the side of my chest
where the steam was letting itself out,
out of my big family chest.
From the dusk to the dawn of nighttime in my body.
yeah
It's like looking into the wrong end of a telescope.
mmmm
I find my light and when I turn it on,
my night demons scatter,
just in time.
huh
oh
My face on your chest
waking up the pigeons in my shaftway,
they start fluttering and cooing thinking it's dawn.
Have you ever seen a baby pigeon?
They are ugly and they make this squealing noise.
I have to admit that I held my breath
and I took chopsticks
and pushed the freshly laid eggs down the shaftway
and the mother pigeon started cooing at my window
and for three days she tortured me
by strutting back and forth on the window ledge,
not that I don't know what it's like to lose eggs,
I tell her.
I'm a killer in the night,
'cause I kill living pigeon eggs,
and I kill roaches with my bare hands.
I sit and watch light move and let it soothe me.
I place my body in the light.

I use this time to accept my whiteness.
I arrange the objects in the room to keep from pacing.
I see the reflection of the night sky in all my stuff.
I go down to the place that baffles me.
I don't want to explain anything anymore.
I'm not afraid.
I want the truth.
Want true love in details.
I'm not satisfied with generalities now that time is passing so fast.
For details I need lots of light.
I want to be loved in fluorescent light.
I love the way it comes on kinda slow,
not right away, and then pops on all of a sudden.
It's so bright and it hums so loud
and it's cheap.
Cheap in a cheap light without shadows;
that's how I want to be loved.
I wanna be in a fluorescent hallway . . .
I wanna be naked in that kinda blue, flickering,
kinda ugly exposed feeling of that cheap hallway light.
I want to be loved in this light
that shows the lumps in my legs
and the stretch marks on my belly,
'cause then I'll know I've been loved.
I want to be loved in cheap light.
My love is cheap, I make it as cheap as I can.
It's sexy to see the truth.
Blue veins under my skin is a real turn-on.
I wish I could hold time still,
just lift it up to that tube of bright fluorescent light
to examine it . . .
I'm going to feel all the emotions I've postponed so far in my life
I'll just go slow,
There's time.
My mother dreamt a tiger was chasing her for 35 years.
Even a roller coaster stops once in a while

when there's no one to ride it.
I hear the ocean rhythm like a breath.
Almost like dreaming without sleeping.
huh
I wake up with a start when I hear a seagull in my shaftway
huh
yeah
I feel delicate like a piece of wood
worn smooth from the motion of the water.

(Peggy gets her gentlemanly self back together. She fixes her tie, tucks in her shirt, and wipes the sweat from her brow.)

All washed up is a better way to describe it.
All washed up and over the hill. Who am I kidding?
I'm afraid I look like a middle-aged guy
who wears his pants too tight
and his shirt is too loud
and who's like an anachronism.
Also the kinda guy
who has to have his belly sticking out over his belt.
I'm never sure if I should put my belly above
or below my belt.
When I gave up cigarettes
I told myself I could have one when I was 86
so I wouldn't be overwhelmed by the loneliness
or the meaninglessness of life. The first year
I found it impossible to watch a sunset
'cause it made no sense without a cigarette.
The heat of the smoke in my lungs made me feel less alone.
I always thought if I really wanted to pass as a man,
it wouldn't be all that difficult:
I would just shave the top of my head in a bald spot
and let the sides softly grow out . . .
You'd tell me if I was looking foolish wouldn't you?
Would you still desire me if I got Alzheimer's?

Of course you would.
Of course you would.
Of course you think in the future
you will feel the same as the present.
Of course you do.
Of course you do.
How can I break the news to you.
I was a meteor once.
I was a meteor who landed in a hillside
In Northern Ireland
Zip zip me up, mop me
on the street I'm on the outside
like a tiger on the inside
sweating in the cold
missing you in a . . . French way . . .
Bon jour, croissant, coupe de ville

(Sings song in the style of Jacques Brel's "Ne Me Quitte Pas" in a tongue-in-cheek French romantic fashion. Music continues under spoken part.)

I can lift still.
I can leave if I want to.
I can turn
I can say goodbye and go,
anything
I can yell to you across the street
Through the traffic
You've already gone and you're not turning around
You used to turn around till you couldn't see me any more.
My brother and sister came to see me in Times Square
and when they left
I waved to them 'til they disappeared
around the corner of 53rd Street.
The last time I saw my mother
I waved to her out of the window of the car
until she was no longer in my vision.

The next day they called me
and told me she wouldn't make it through the night.
Goodbyes dribble out of my mouth.
I drool on the sidewalk after you're gone.
They'll find me here years later,
they'll find me yelling and waving through the
trucks and the busses,
and the cars and the traffic, over and over,
joining all the spirits they walt disneyed over in Times Square.
If you were young and clapped at the sun setting every night
they would think it was touching and romantic.
If you're old and do the same things
they think you're crazy.
Goodbyes dripping over my lips.
Just seeing you I yelled out in front of everyone.
Stupid, sexy breathing songs—like
mmmmmmmmmmmm
I'd love to love you baby.
I can yell to you across the street.
Through the traffic
You've already gone. You're not turning around.
You used to turn around over and over again
till you couldn't see me anymore.
What time is it?
I don't remember because every time I try, tears come.
I no longer care what anybody thinks.
I used to care,
I remember the day I heard my heart move
into a position in my body I didn't recognize.
Almost like when you're screwing a cap on a bottle
and it won't go and then it does.
Or you find the grooves on a zip-lock bag.
That's what happened to my insides.

(Still talking over the music.)

I will make a new language
with words that will adequately describe my love for you.
I will make a land where there is only love.
I will buy you a house!
And stand outside
and protect you from everything bad
that could ever happen to you.
I will take you to an island
where there is a dormant volcano
and it will rise up again.
And fire will shoot out of little holes in the ground
next to our feet as we walk down the street.
I will do anything
Please don't go
I will be the shadow of your shadow
the shadow of your hand
the shadow of your dog
Don't leave me . . . don't leave me . . . don't leave me.

(The music ends.)

Every Saturday night
I strap my breasts down
and get a haircut
and I dress up in a fancy suit with cufflinks
and a tie clip and a tie and polished shoes,
I'm all shiny shiny.
I wear a flower in my lapel
and cologne splashed on my cheeks
and am paid $500 to take the same woman out dancing.
I've been doing this for the last twenty years.
I pick her up in a rented car
and get out and open the door for her.
She blushes
and says how lovely it is to find such a gentleman.

I tell her how beautiful she is
when she gets that red streak across her cheek
and she says that was the reason her first husband married her.
Every Saturday afternoon
I want to give it up,
but I can't because of the money of course.
I also think somewhere
I really enjoy being her fancy gentleman
and I can spend an entire evening
not having to decide which toilet to use.
I think somewhere she loves me.
I always show her safely to the door
and kiss her goodnight
and say how attracted to her I am
but I would never consider doing anything about it
because I have such a deep respect for her
and maybe after we get to know each other better
we can talk about it.
She blushes again
and puts the door between us
and says that's probably best for right now.
I reluctantly leave
and tell her it will feel like an eternity
till I see her again.

(As if waiting for someone, speaks a song in the style of Nina Simone's "Turn Me On.")

(Fade slowly and sadly to black.)

The Big Lie

I cracked open an egg
that vibrated the stove back and forth so hard
it created an earthquake that rattled the kitchen
till it shut off all the electricity below 14th Street
and set off every smoke alarm
in every apartment downtown.
The aftershock was so great
it flung my neighbor out of his third story window
and before his body hit the pavement
the sidewalk cracked open so wide
that his body kept going down
into the sparking electric wires
that were lighting up the sewers
under the streets of New York
and the rats and the artists and the vendors
that the mayor was hiding down there
were electrocuted in such a loud crack
that it shut all the museums
and woke up millions of Wall Street workers
who had occupied the neighborhood
and they were flung out of their windows
so scared that they were yelling
do you have any life insurance

From *It's a Small House and We Lived in it Always* by Split Britches in collaboration with Clod Ensemble, 1999.

out of their car windows
until their Volvos rained down like meteor showers
and sent the Circle Line boats up the river backwards
and the tourists saw all the surplus money
in the richest government in the world
go up the president's nose
and out the mayor's cold ass
which froze the Hudson River
and Walt Disney's proclamation
that all men are created equal was shattered
like millions of icicles against the Statue of Liberty
which sent the rents soaring so high
that I saw the southern cross in the north
and the northern star in the south
and the Aurora Borealis
and the constellations in the morning
were indistinguishable from one another
Until Orion's Belt was lined up with Mars
to give me a small feeling of what it looks like
when death rips a thirty-eight-year-old friend
at the prime of his life and the height of his talent
and flings him against his will and in front of my eyes
into the fires on the other side
not a pretty sight as hard as it is to die
Which reminds me
When the United States Constitution was written
95% of all Americans were either slaves or indentured servants.
Yeah
Can't wait to see the video.

To My Chagrin
Written by Peggy Shaw
In collaboration with Vivian Stoll
Edited and directed by Lois Weaver
Performed with Vivian Stoll

To My Chagrin was first performed at Jump Start, in San Antonio, in 2001, where it was directed by Steve Bailey. It was subsequently performed at the Off Center in Austin, Texas, and then at PS122 in New York, where it was directed by Lois Weaver.

"Sterling's Poem for Peggy on Opening Night of To My Chagrin*"*

You are the real strength of America—
Not the self-imagined strength of regimented flags and anthems
But the actual nation of mixed and broken pieces,
Tied and re-woven together,
Multi-colored strands twisted and knotted
for maximum endurance.
Mixed-up and broken chunks of identity, repaired and re-used
Better than new
Stronger than ever
Dense and impenetrable as dreadlocks.
Outcasts own everything, and you are as rich as Midas
as rich as Elvis rich
As dead Otis and Sam Cooke,
rich enough to purchase resurrection
From the wreckage.

STERLING HOUSTON (1945–2006)
SAN ANTONIO, OCTOBER 26, 2001

To My Chagrin

(The stage is set with an old pickup truck that has been cut in half. The cab of the truck is stage right, facing forward with the driver side door opened. The bed of the truck is stage left with the back end facing toward the audience. Inside the bed is a partially assembled drumset. Other parts of the drumset are scattered outside of the truck, some sitting on a dolly by its side.)

(Pre-show music in the style of Chuck Berry and Otis Redding plays.)

(Viv, the drummer, enters with a stick bag and a cymbal bag. She lays the cymbal bag against the bed of the truck, then goes to the cab of the truck, enters the driver's side door and turns on the radio.)

(Viv goes to the bed of the truck and starts to set up the drums: cymbal stands, tom, cymbals, snare. When she is seated on the drum stool, she takes the hi-hat clip from the hi-hat stand. Pre-show music fades out. The blinker light on the bed of the truck starts blinking simultaneously and we hear the blinker light's sound.)

(Peggy enters from back of audience.)

I heard that Sam Cooke was killed in his underwear
in a motel room.
Did you hear that?
I know he wore white boxer shorts.

Marvin Gaye was killed by his father
in an argument in his own home.

One of the Supremes was found in a welfare motel
in Washington or Philadelphia
Or was it Detroit?
In a single room.
Is that true?

Did Marvin Gaye's father really kill him?
I know that Malcolm X's grandson set his
Grandmother's house on fire.
She died of burns three weeks later.

I know that Otis Redding is dead.
I remember the day he died.
I was brushing my teeth and I couldn't
Put the two sides of my life back together without him.
So I switched to James Brown and Wilson Pickett.

Little Black Sambo was the only black boy I knew till 8th grade.

In 1957, I was a missionary to Central America, teaching perfectly
Happy Catholics how to be Protestants.

Bessie Smith died 'cause they wouldn't treat her at a white-only
hospital emergency room. They turned her away.
Or was it Billie Holiday?
Your lips are too small to play the trumpet,
they told Louis Armstrong.
I was lucky I didn't believe anything I was told.
I thought I was Scottish till my father died and everyone at the
funeral was Irish.

See the USA
In your Chevrolet.

I was told that Dinah Shore had defective genes that caused her to
Give birth to two black children in a row.

(Viv plays drumbeat. Peggy and Viv sing.)

Fa fa fa fa fa fa fa fa fa.

Houdini died 'cause after a show someone punched him in the
stomach and he didn't have time to tense his muscles.
It's like renovation—gut renovation.
It can catch you by surprise.
It can kill you.

(The blinker light stops blinking. Viv plays drumbeat. Peggy and Viv sing.)

Fa fa fa fa fa fa fa fa.

Otis Redding has always been a backdrop to my emotions
He died too soon in a plane crash like all good singers.
And he's still dead.

Nothing here goes together, it doesn't mesh.
The music doesn't go with the walls, the furniture doesn't
Go with the people, the windows look out into the wrong
Place.

I feel like I'm in the home of somebody's relatives and
They're not sure they want me here, kind of like they're
Acting like they're running a restaurant and I'm acting like
I'm in it but I'm really in a house somewhere
Pretending to be in Manhattan
pretending to be in a rock 'n' roll band.

I'm not pretending to make sense.
I'm mature now and I'm dirty. Just from living.
And graying at the temples. My hair seems dirty to me

When it gets gray.

Time flies, then you go back to the silence you came from
Before you were born. Where was that now?
Oh, yeah. Down with the roots of trees.
Quiet like when
You turn off the ignition after a long hard drive.

*(Peggy rests her hand on the truck cab. Music/dance number. Loud mixed
sound effects in the style of Chuck Berry's "No Particular Place to Go,"
accompanied by live drums. Peggy tumbles and rolls over the truck hood and
cab. The truck seems alive with lights coming from inside and underneath as
Peggy crashes and dives. She eventually tries to open the door, can't get it
open, while Viv simultaneously plays beats on drum. Peggy looks at Viv,
realizes the door is locked, unlocks it and opens the door, which releases the
number into a rhythmic dance in the style of Chuck Berry, with the open door
in a spotlight, using the door like a guitar and a dance partner. It ends with
Peggy holding the door as a guitar to fading vibrations as she says next line.)*

Did you know that every day in New York City,
Harry Belafonte asks people he doesn't know in the
back seat of a taxi
to buckle up?

(Peggy slams the car door as Viv hits a loud drum crash.)

I woke up early with summer gray hair that came on
Overnight looking a lot like Richard Gere.
I went into the kitchen.
There you were my grand-companion-son.
You were staring out the window
Into the backyard. In the night, the wind had blown down
A 150-year-old groovy tree that was so big it smashed
Across six backyards including mine.

It left a hole in the sky where it had been for so long and
The light smashed into the kitchen
where it had never been before.
Its branches scratched the side door of my backyard '71
Torino as it fell. I was shocked that I hadn't heard it.
Maybe I do fall asleep sometimes in the night.
The tree ripped up a huge circle right out of the ground that
went down about 20 feet
and next to it was a 20 foot high mound of dirt
full of roots wrapped around rocks.
It looked brand new.
The contents of the hole were exposed to us in full view.

And then there was the hole itself.

*(Peggy opens door—starts to sing a song in the style of "No Particular Place
to Go." Viv continues to play then realizes Peggy is not continuing. Drums
slow down and get quieter.)*

We went outside together without talking.
We got close to it.
We smelled the dirt and it seemed familiar.
I took off my clothes. You got real quiet.

*(The drums soften into a jazz waltz pattern. Peggy's back is to the audience.
She slowly removes her jacket.)*

I think it was the way I took my clothes off combined with
The shock of the tree falling that alerted you that
Something had changed.
With no clothes, and through your eyes, my body felt
Very feminine, very soft, and very naked.

(Drums stop.)

I looked at the tree
Something about it looked . . . big and
Sad and helpless and down like a dead elephant.
I felt as if I was going to spring up into the hole in the sky
the tree had left.
Instead, at that moment, I got in.

(Peggy gets into the truck.)

How could I pass up this opportunity of a hole?
You said you'd help me.
You started shoveling heavy wet dirt
on my white cold body.
I thought I'd freak out. But the dirt smelled so
Familiar, like I'd been there before. Me and the dead
Tree. Getting dirty. Old and dirty.

When I was covered up to my neck, you said I looked like a
Flower growing in the woods where the tree had been.
You built a fire.
I watched the fire.
We both kept watch over the tree.

I heard it breathing, slowly, like it was dying.
It made faces. One had a tongue sticking out.
One was laughing and
Another was howling . . .
I heard animal footsteps in the yard. I heard leaves
Crackling way down the street. I thought, this is something
Unique to being in the ground.

(Peggy speak-sings to a song in the style of Screamin' Jay Hawkins's "I Hear Voices," while she sits in the cab of the truck.)

I dreamt about Jamaica

I smelled your hair
I saw the hole in the ground where you were born
I thought I'd find you there
The shadows are full of chagrin
You were young and dark
And I had a 1959 Cadillac Coupe de Ville
With a key to the gas tank.
I don't stand a chance
In this missing kind of dance
Most love is a burden
I think I just want romance
I can't win
I'm growin' old while you're sleepin'
I'm dying till I see you again
You asked me how big is a heart
I say about 350 cc's
I laugh
I have to laugh
I'm movin' fast but
I'm runnin' out of gas
I've been here too long
You're waiting for me
Just down the road
I feel something climbing up my spine
My heart is stuck in my throat
I'm calling your name
I'm not answering the phone
I can't find my glasses
I see fake flowers everywhere
I see Chinese wind chimes hangin' down
I see the Virgin of Guadalupe

(Peggy collapses, head down, drumming stops.)

I'm lost . . . in the wilderness . . .

(Viv starts drumbeat again. Peggy steps out of truck cab, leaves arm on door, and speak-sings a song in the style of "It was a Very Good Year." Peggy collapses again, melting, arm grasps door of truck, again drumming fades and stops.)

I'm lost . . . in bitterness . . .

(Viv starts drumming again. Peggy moves out from behind door. Peggy signals Viv to stop drumming and come over to her. Viv climbs out of the truck bed, comes up behind Peggy and wraps her jacket around her shoulders. Peggy wiggles out of it and moves upstage. Viv throws the jacket onto the truck door and returns to the drums.)

(Viv starts drumbeat again. Peggy falls to her knees expecting Viv to stop drumming and assist her. Viv refuses to help or stop drumming. Peggy tries again. Viv still refuses and continues to play for a few moments. Peggy moves to a sitting position, arms wrapped around her knees. Viv plays more softly.)

My mouth opened, my lips parted like they hadn't moved
In a long time.
I was silent. I closed my eyes, and I was falling through
Sparkle dust, falling into a pile of clothes at my feet.
I was naked in front of everyone I knew.
Naked except for my white boxer shorts and white shoes
And socks.

A voice inside me told me I was beautiful.
It also told me I'd be here for a while.

(Viv stops drumming.)

The generator was on but the lines were down.
We'll have to sit here till the power comes back on.

We started talking.

(Viv hits sticks on the snare, stopping when she talks but playing through Peggy's lines.)

VIV:
I don't like hard shapes.

PEGGY:
I didn't understand you and I said
Heart shapes?
And you said no . . .

VIV:
Hard shapes, like wood is hard.

PEGGY:
So you like soft shapes, like circles.

VIV:
Yeah, but I don't like squares.

(Viv hits the snare drum, then clicks the sticks together as she climbs out of the back of the truck bed and walks around to the side.)

PEGGY:
You said, "I'll tell you all my bad dreams
but I can't tell the good ones
If I keep them to myself no one can take them away
And my dream will come true."

VIV:
Sometimes I only tell you half my dream
'cause the other half is good.
That keeps you from knowing everything about me.
That's good in a relationship.

(Hits truck cab with sticks.)

PEGGY:

As opposed to cars
It's good to know everything about cars
Like if they've been in an accident
Or had new transmissions

(Peggy slides under the cab of the truck on the dolly while Viv plays a rhythmic solo on the roof, windshield, and hood. Viv finishes playing as Peggy slides out onto the other side of the truck and pulls herself up.)

I was supposed to be a soft shape
But I didn't stick around for soft
I thought soft would keep me safe and cozy
When I should be out being hard
Fighting wars
To protect my mom
Or my girlfriend who was soft.

(Viv plays a beat loudly on the roof of the truck with the back side of the sticks, then stops.)

VIV:

I suppose you think you know what masculine is.

PEGGY:

(Very femme pose and voice.)
I have been accused of being masculine
I would like to talk to you about that.
About passing on my masculinity
I got my big Adam's apple from my dad *(Drum hit.)*
It's bigger than James Dean's. *(Hit.)*
I've had a lot of experience being man enough . . .
Butch enough . . .

And fast.
I've been a King *(Hit.)* a Drag *(Hit.)* a Racist *(Hit.)*
A He-man *(Hit.)* and a Confessor.

(Viv hits truck with sticks until she reaches Peggy and puts her right stick on Peggy's left shoulder.)

VIV:
Do you have a confession to make?

PEGGY:
I moved to New York City
I left my barber in Santa Fe
I got a good haircut
In Brooklyn the other day
I'm always on the move
No place to call my own
I got back to New York City—
And I noticed my hair had grown—
Short on the sides
Flat on the top
Fade up the back.
I got a great haircut
Back in Santa Fe
She didn't ask me questions
She just cut hair all day.

(Viv starts swing jazz beat on the drums. Peggy starts singing her song, "The Flattop Blues.")

I got the gotta get a flattop
No backtalk barber blues
I said I got the gotta get a flattop
No backtalk barber blues
It's worth a trip from New York City

I know it's just my hair I'll lose.
My hair's long gone
I left it on the floor
My hair's long gone
I left it on the floor
They swept it up in Houston
In a haircut store.
I got 56 children
I raise boys and girls the same
I got 56 children
I raise boys and girls the same
I give 'em all buzz cuts
Shave their hair right down to the brain.
I got a he/she barber
She really knows how to cut.
I got a he/she barber
He really knows how to cut.
Well, she took a trip to San Francisco
And now he's back to strut his stuff.

I was pissing into the cold stony tree dirt like my old cars
Leaking in the driveway.
No fancy suit, no silk tie to protect me . . .
Just dirty.
No polished shoes.
No hair products.
No attitude.

VIV:
No balls!

PEGGY:
Just my head appearing to the world where the tree had been.
I began to wish I had left last night
before the tree was blown down.

It felt good to think about the weather.

You know what always makes me feel better
is thinking about all the cars I've owned
and picturing them right after I washed them
and the sun is reflecting off the steel and chrome.

(Singing/talking.)

Like my first car . . .
A 1951 Plymouth Electroglide. Torquoise and white.
Then I had a 1961 VW Bus. Light green and white.
A 1962 Pontiac Catalina. Blue with black hardtop.
A 1979 red and white VW camper bus.
1971 Ford Torino, still in my yard.
1973 Buick Apollo. Gold with brown hardtop.
1973 Chevy Malibu. Green.
A 1981 Datsun truck. Red.
A 1974 blue Ford station wagon.
I have a passion for cars.

Passion-less is a word I would use to describe my state of mind:
Undriven, like my old cars sitting in the backyard. Unmotivated.
Like a bad exhaust system. Dull. Thick, like L.A. smog.
Trying not to use the word old.
Or vintage.
Can't seem to get excited about much of anything.
Only the memory of what cars mean.

You know what I mean?

I'll go outside and sit in a car.
I'm not afraid to die.
I'm not afraid of being alone.
I'll sit in the driver's seat.

I'll pick at rust spots.
I spit out the window.
I stick shift.
I'm alone.
I squeeze my face in the rear view mirror.
I think I see the reflection of a passing car hood but it's light
Flashing in the corner of my eye. I have to sit down.
The doctor said
It's either too much coffee or not enough . . . Cars.

I think I'm relaxed but my ears move when I don't realize it.
I think I'm being really still and my jaw clenches.
My aunt's jaw used to clench and unclench like my
Grandfather's, but I don't let myself think of my aunt too much.
Not on purpose, just 'cause time moves in a line.
We had a lot of time together once. We won't again.
I miss her. She was killed by a drunk driver in a 1955 red T-Bird
Convertible 33 years ago
When she went out for a bottle of milk . . .

And she's still dead.
Like my old cars leaking in the driveway.

How can I tell you how I feel about my cars?

(Peggy sings.)

I got a Torino
And a Cadillac
I got 56 cars
Right out back
They got no plates
And they won't start
But you never know when you might need a part.

Cars all around the yard
And up a tree
Cars are everywhere
Just thrilling me.

I bulldoze the yard once a week
I shift the corpses
To make room for me

I got carburetors
I got tires too
I got hoods
Engines
Seat belts
Bucket seats
Bank seats
Dual exhausts
Fluid drive
Overdrive
Transmissions
Gas gauge
Full serve
Self-serve
Gas-guzzler
Cold start
Car chase
Anti-lock
Anti-life
Anti-Christ
Fill 'er up
Foot to the floor
Smokin'
Cranking
Revving

Back to the wall!

I feel like my stand on things
is getting all mushy and watered down.
Down in my maturity.
Thank God with this amount of testosterone I'll never have balls.
What does wishy-washy really mean anyway?

VIV:
No balls.

PEGGY:
You're lucky you were born at a time when girls could *play* drums.
I was brought way up in a place
Where no one trusted any girl who drove fast.

(Viv starts drumbeat as if starting a race competition. The drums get slowly faster and faster over the next sequence.)

But I drove very very fast outta that lonesome town
I drove straight through fill 'er ups.
Bathroom visits only.

VIV:
Son of a bitch!

PEGGY:
Now I'm hauling ass.
I'm in the next county already.

VIV:
Whew!

PEGGY:
I'm not giving up the wheel easy

And I'm not stopping for a Coca-Cola.

VIV:
This dude's cookin' with gas all right!

PEGGY:
I corner good too.

VIV:
No shit!

PEGGY:
I push that pedal to the floor.

VIV:
Whoa, 155 on an open road!

(The drumbeat has reached a very fast rhythm and with the bass drum added becomes a full rock 'n' roll beat. Peggy starts singing a rock 'n' roll song in the style of Chuck Berry's "Maybelline.")

And then a sound. I could barely hear it.
Almost like it wasn't really supposed to be heard.
It was a young voice, deep and tender, and moist and dark,
And full of love.
Suddenly the tree looked decayed.
Almost abandoned
like the part of the subway tunnel near 4th Street
Where there was a single light bulb swinging back and forth
And casting eerie shadows on the walls.

(Viv starts fast drumbeat from before. Getting faster and faster as Peggy speaks.)

Then I see you just in time.

I swerve, skid, kid,
Brake fast, roll my eyes
And there you are!
My premature grandbaby lilac son!
You came flying out of your mama's garage
Right onto my wrong side of the road.

I pull over and think to myself
Isn't he lovely.
Isn't he beautiful.

A pretty shade of lilac you were
A lilac baby with leopard upholstery and
Mixed
Race stripes
Racing stripes
Mixed spots
On your rear end

You saw me first thing
Like the sitting duck that I was
When your crown came through that hole
I knew right away you'd be royalty
And fast like me
I could tell
You were a chip off the old block
My car was idling waiting for you to get in.
Vroom vroom vroom
Your little 8-cylinder engine kicked in
Humming
Purring like a kitten.

(Talk-singing.)

You're my mixed grandbaby

There ain't no other way.
I'm your butch grandmama
With way too much to say
You keep acting like me . . .

I'm gonna . . .

Ooh aah ooh aah cool cool kitty
Tell us about the boy from New York City.

(Drums end.)

(Talking.)

Now you want me to tell you too much and go too far
What if I can't get back in time

All I can tell you is what I know

I'm pale I'm all white next to you
I pale in comparison
I'm an inbred white bread
Except for my brown left arm hanging out the car window
From driving right close to the sun

White people like me are all inbred
I know that for a fact
All white people in America are descended from criminals
And religious fanatics
That's who came to the original Thanksgiving

My hand is so much bigger than yours
For now
And so much whiter
We compare hands

We contrast our hands
We take pictures of our hands

Where's the race? You asked

I turn off the engine
I put my arm on the back of the seat
My son of grand I tell you
My ex-husband, your grand slam father
Is proven by Hitlerguy
To come from
Ten generations of pure white Ger-man

Your white mother, my daughter
Put an end to that his story
She is the daughter of a couple mixed
Queer mother me and heterosexual dad father him

I'm a mixed up second generation
First cousin combo
Inbred Irish grand-butch-mother

You're my dual-heritage, bi-racial, mixed metaphor,
Well-bred, bye-bye, sweet island boy.

(Peggy unbuttons her shirt. A video of her grandson, Ian, is projected onto her bare chest.)

How can I explain to you how I feel about teaching you to drive?

(To Viv's drum beat, Peggy speak-sings an original song called "Driving While Black.")

You gotta put both hands on the wheel
for what I'm about to tell you.

Cold, it's so cold what I'm about to say.
So cold you could freeze to death.

Keep your hands on the steering wheel.
Keep your hands in sight.
No hands in pockets.
No hands moving.
No hands in motion.
Do you want me to be like you when I grow up? you said.
I know what I don't want you to be.
But I can't tell you.

No inmate
No criminal
No cop
No illegal immigrant
No soldier
No basketball player

You gotta buckle up for what I'm about to tell you
Cold, it's so cold what I'm about to say.
So cold you could freeze to death.
Do not move
If you move you're over
You could die if you move.
You could be killed for moving.
Don't reach for anything you could be killed for.
Do you want me to be like you? you said.
I know what I don't want you to be
But I'd never tell you.

No politician
No lawyer
No doctor
No CEO

No Secretary of State
No Director of Homeland Security

So stop
Be silent
Be still
You have the right to remain silent.

Not in a junkyard
Not in the White House
Not on Broadway

Not in a deadend job
Not in the newspaper
Not on death row

You gotta get out of the car and keep your hands up
Spread your legs.
You have the right to remain silent,
Silent, frozen and cold.

I'm trying to explain to you how on a cold morning
You go outside
Say a prayer, pump the gas once and turn it over.

I suddenly came back to where I was
You had my Torino headlights shining on me.
The ground where the tree had been wanted me out.
The tree gave me a knowing look and
A shove. Better do what the ground says, the ground
Knows, you said. I made a sharp sound and my eyes got
Moist like when you hit the bridge of your nose.
I yelled for you to hurry and dig me out.
I was suffocating.
You were digging your frantic fingers into my dirt.
It seemed to take forever and the dirt was so heavy and

There was so much of it. When you finally got my arms
Uncovered you yanked me out of the ground. I was out
With such speed and feeling that you could see my marks
On the fallen tree as I went by; like leaving rubber. The air
Was so cold after the dirt, so cold that there was a column
Of smoke rising off my white body into the night.
You gasped at the sight.
I wanted to go back into the ground.
But you wrapped me in blankets and held me tight like a
New-born babe. You held me up high,
like an offering to the hole in the sky.
It's a Butch!
I'm sure of it, you said.
It's a girl, a big butch girl,
you yelled to the fallen
Tree and my old Torino and the fire. The tree died and you
Lived! You said. The tree sacrificed itself for you!

(Viv performs a beautiful drum solo.)

I was under the impression that life was a progression.

VIV:
In western tonal music, a progression is simply a series of chords
traveling through time, creating sensations of tension and release.
Every chord has a particular function depending on its context.
The dominant chord as a half cadence
is the greatest point of tension
because it longs with all its heart
to reach the final resolution and rest.
But this is only functional harmony . . .
sometimes a chord is just a chord.

PEGGY:
I'm sorry for the part I have played in the amount of cars
There are in the world.

I have confessed and named them all.
Just the smell of them makes my heart beat faster.
I've left them lying in my
Backyard garden of used parts.
Like Detroit
Don't forget the Motor City.

(Peggy and Viv sing.)

Fa fa fa fa fa fa fa fa fa.

I heard the first freeway in America
Was driven right through
The middle of Detroit.
Dividing the city forever
Ford on the right
Motown on the left.
Did you hear that?
Is that true?

Then Ford took flight and left
All the buildings to rot
Now all the pheasants and foxes have come back
And everyone else is driving by,
Just passing by the not-so-free-way.
Did you hear that?

(Peggy and Viv sing.)

Fa fa fa fa fa fa fa fa.

I always said I wouldn't trust anyone
Who didn't remember JFK being shot.
I revise that statement
to people who don't know what a carburetor is.

(Blinker on bed of truck starts. Viv starts packing up sticks.)

I thought Bobby Kennedy was gonna plant a tree on every block.
Instead, just before they killed him,
He opened an FBI file on James Baldwin
Is that true?

I thought Colin Powell was going to be the first
Black president of the United States . . .

I know George Bush's son gave all the forests away to his friends.
Did you hear that?

I'm gonna plant you a weeping willow tree my son of grand
And I'm gonna plant a tree for every Republican in this country
I'm gonna name the trees by their personal names
I'm gonna make little bronze plaques
Like seats in a church
Then they won't cut them down.

There'll be a Cheney cherry
A Kissinger willow
An oak tree named Ashcroft, a pine tree named Rumsfeld
A maple tree named Donald Trump
On the west side
And then he won't cut it down
In 50 years when you're my age, the weeping willow tree will be
Grown and you can sit in the shadow and rest.

(Viv gets up and walks to the truck cab. The truck's blinkers stop. Viv leans inside truck and fiddles with the radio. A recording of Ian's voice is heard from inside the truck. Viv gives Peggy a nod and exits.)

(With Ian's voice.)

Light-skinned cognac, not-so-late-at-night rhythm.

My island, mine, mind your eyes and ears youngsta
Deep-tanned way out in the grass that moves feeling
Love life, love you, love the way you walk always
So gone, way gone, underneath the stars kinda
Shadows, details, lighting up your face.
Naked, back view, showing who you're talking to
Dubbed-in, voices, not the way it was, really
Slow down, meditate,
Concentrate, lay back, let your ears relax
Listen to the love music
Love child, not legal, hidden in the woods, baby
Hot-spot, 5-spot, love you in the right place

Moving gently to bring you the news
It keeps me—gives me the best of both worlds
You beat me, you beat me to it
In public, in private moments, gotta listen to hearts
Way under, way over, sailing through waves
My shadow, my outline, doesn't change all the years
Teaching and teaching gotta teach you to teach
I gotta hurry and hurry to tell you
Crossing uncrossing, you're darka, you're darka
Half-freed, mixed up mista bebop boogie woogie.

*(A typically fast rock 'n' roll song in the style of James Brown's "I Feel Good,"
for example, is sung slowly, like a ballad, as though Black music were being
made white.)*

I'm back in the kitchen now
and you're still staring out the window
I open the window and my eyes don't adjust to the light
I'm blinded by morning
I'm blinded white

It's bright, it's white
So much white in my head

You're kinda bright dark
Dark
Blinded by shadows
Your shadows are so bright
Blinded by night

I feel good
'cause I got you.

(Peggy gets into the truck cab, rolls up the windows, adjusts the mirror, and locks the doors. She is putting the truck to sleep.)

(The music plays out, while Peggy exits.)

Blue

I am so low
That's how down I am
Way down
Like at the bottom of the sea
Where the fish have no eyes
Way down
Like in the Southern Hemisphere where the moon is on top
And the water goes the wrong way around
Down
It is so dark down here a sunrise has never been seen
They call it the sea of love
I don't call it the sea of love.

Mmmmmmmmmmmmmmmm
Bluuuue's how ya feel
Bluuue's
How ya feeeeel
Mmm mmmm mmm

I'm down in a basement somewhere
The window's above my head
I see feet walking by
Cause I'm laying back in my bed
There's mold growing in the fireplace
And the rug is wet underneath
I think it's you I can taste
But I can't get on my feet
What a waste
Take your shoes off outside
So you don't step on my heart and wake my mama

From *It's a Small House and We Lived in It Always,* by Split Britches, in collaboration with Clod Ensemble, 1999.

When you live in one place too long you start
Living with your parents and looking like your pets
Hey
Don't turn on the light
'Cause I am no sight
For day or night
I remember you
Déjà vu

I'm so down
On the ground
I'm so dog-gone down
That's how down
I am
Blue's how ya feel
Blue's how ya feel
Blue

MUST—THE INSIDE STORY

Must—The Inside Story
Peggy Shaw in collaboration with Clod Ensemble
By Peggy Shaw and Suzy Willson
Must was first performed at the Wellcome Collection in London,
November 2008
Performed by Peggy Shaw
Directed by Suzy Willson
Original music by Paul Clark
Lighting by Hansjörg Schmidt
Design by Sarah Blenkinsop
Violin: Calina de la Mare
Piano: John Paul Gandy
Double Bass: Lucy Shaw
Produced by Fuel
Supported by the Wellcome Trust and Arts Council England

Clod Ensemble (www.clodensemble.com) is a performance company based in London, led by artistic directors Paul Clark and
Suzy Willson. Music and movement are at the heart of all the
company's work. Productions include *Red Ladies* (ICA, Serralves
Museum, Portugal, 2008) and *Under Glass* (Sadlers Wells, London,
2009). *Must* was created as part of the company's award-winning
Performing Medicine program (www.performingmedicine.com),
which uses the arts to teach medical students and practicing
health professionals. Since 2008, it has toured medical schools
and theaters around the world, including Barts and the London
School of Medicine, Edinburgh University's Anatomy Theatre, the
New York Shakespeare Festival Public Theatre Under the Radar
Festival, and Soho Theatre, London. *Must* is performed with a live
band consisting of piano, double bass, and violin, and features a

backdrop of microphotographs of the inside of a body, courtesy of the Wellcome Image Library.

"Our bodies are ceaselessly changing.
What we were yesterday and are today,
we will not be tomorrow."
—Ovid, *The Metamorphoses* (8 A.D.)

"Change is gonna come."
—Sam Cooke (1964)

Must—The Inside Story

Prelude

I've been waiting for you
and now you're here.

I am descended
from a long line of pachyderms.
I'm a non ruminate undulate,
Thick-skinned *Elephas Maximus.*
I am not sensitive to criticism or ridicule.

I know one thing.
(It's always good to know one thing.)
I'm a Lover.
Mama was. Papa was too.

Come with me.

I am falling over the balcony
into the orchestra.
The walls are made of red curtains,
but they're not curtains at all.
They are blood vessels
carved to look like curtains.
What do you think happened?
Who turned on the light?

One

When my skin cracks open
You will find my meat.
My carnivore body.

You will see the anthills and mole tunnels underground and food
being carried from place to place by millions of workers. You will
see a magical landscape, like New York City in the seventies—
finding graffiti and layers of bone and blood and sex shops and
garbage.

You will see two skeletons holding each other in the desert and a
giant in Mongolia who can remove plastic from dolphins'
stomachs with his hands down their throats, 'cause his arms are
forty seven inches long. Evidence that someone lives in here.
Really lives here and leaves traces.

The tips of my fingers trace you on a foggy window. They trace
your outline and they make a heart with an arrow through it.
Such a simple map showing the pain of an arrow through the
heart, explaining that feeling when you have something outside
of yourself that draws you to it—like a crash at the front of the
bus, or a commotion outside the square, like blood cells rushing
to an injured place where they desert the rest of your body and
leave you exhausted.

I keep finding the future inside of me. I can hear it really loud,
coming like a field of windmills, or a hive of bees.

I know, I know, I know.

I am digging. Deep past the topsoil. There's no cutting involved.
Just turning over the soil. I'm afraid of finding something I didn't
know about—like a bear shitting in my woods, or a field of Irish

potatoes in my uterus, or a huge, garbage-swirling, plastic toxic mass in my pituitary gland that is close to the size of Texas. Fish and turtles and things are growing in it and eating it and fossils are traveling on it to foreign dangerous places where they are not meant to be.

My dad used to say my ears were so dirty I could grow potatoes in them. He said if I ate seeds I would grow an orange tree in my belly. He said this feeling of fluttering in my chest is the leaves of an orange tree blowing in a storm. My heart bending with the wind, like his, brushing against my ribs.

The sea is rising, eroding the edges of my flesh, making it soft like silk. I have lost thirty-one square miles of land in thirty years.

My desire is melting my icebergs so fast, they're drifting further and further apart and polar bears are dying from exhaustion.

I'm gonna lay down and make myself small and dig a hole in my back yard and crawl all the way down to my feet. Upside-down in China.

Underneath my thighs is where all the oil is being stolen from, leaving empty pockets inside. The first thing I think of in the morning and the last thing at night, is that my thighs will collapse in on themselves from the huge caverns where the oil used to be.

My shoulders are not the mountains of Tibet—I don't care what you say.

> I have seen the mountains
> and I can breathe above the tree line.

> I am in the habit of trees,
> but I can live without them.

I am not in the habit of you, for sure,
'cause they took you away.

I know, I know I know I know I know,
I know, I know, I know.

Ain't no sunshine when she's gone
Only darkness every day.

Two

It's funny talking to you this way now, as if, in a way, you're a stranger. There was a time when I felt aligned with you, complicit in what we both knew. Now I'm not sure. I'm not sure of anything. I'm just gonna tell you a story, the inside story.

There are different ways of seeing inside me:

You could guess what's in here.
You could x-ray me.
You could touch me.
Or you could believe what I tell you.

You may describe me as someone who is unscrupulous or dishonest. A rogue. I have been described as a biologically inferior variant. I live apart. A bull, a tramp, a vagrant. I spend too much time looking at beautiful ladies. If you look at me from the front you will notice there is a part of my body that you can't put your finger on.

I'm not afraid of you and I'm not afraid of being alone. How do I know I can trust you?

How do I know that you haven't got a gun in your pocket, or a stethoscope?

I feel your fingerprints all over me.

This is a story about time. About coming from the darkness to the light. I always thought time started when I was born and ended when I died. Didn't you? But it all started a long time ago in black and white. And now it's a fact of life. There's no logic in here. No beginning, middle or end.

It's a journey through the shadows of a city. A map. The wrinkles on my face are where the map gets folded over and over.

    It's just a pound of flesh,
    a Book of Love.

    Oh, I wonder, wonder, who wrote
    the Book of Love.

Three

You had a skeleton in your closet until yesterday. I assumed it was a pigeon, but it coulda been a dove.

White delicate bones with wings that folded up against its body like it was resting. Its flesh was just about gone, except a little smell and grey dust that used to be feathers congregated under the skull in a sweet little pile. The beak was closed.

I get brave when someone else is scared.

My body relaxes and becomes like, in balance. I have guts. You say to me,

"You have guts."

I say, my guts are held together by miles of string. But mostly by the belt around my middle and by your fear.

Elephants teach their young to slide their trunks over dead bones. They hold the baby elephants' trunks in theirs, listening as they smooth out the memories.

That's all I could think to do when I saw the pigeon—trace my fingers across the closed beak, the tiny rib cage, the long finger claws.

No more guts or flesh.

Four

My friend, Migdalia Garcia, sucks calcium outta the inside of chicken bones. Then she eats the whole bone. It's sexy—the crunching and sucking of the bones in her mouth. She takes her sweet time, leaves nothing on her plate. I hear her singing outside, she's thinking about bones.

Her bones were flung across Linden Boulevard in Brooklyn in the sixties, when she was in puberty. She flew through the air propelled by a hit-and-run driver. That car smashed all those broken bones across four lanes of highway into a heap on the other side. The driver took off and never knew her name.

Once, while she was crunching bones between her teeth, I fell off a fifteen-foot fence and broke my pelvis and heels. I wouldn't let anyone bring me to a hospital, 'cause I wanted to die at home. Migdalia carried my body up five flights of stairs and slept all night on my floor. The next day, when I wasn't dead, she carried me to the emergency room. While the doctors were telling me I could have died from internal bleeding, she stole all the bandages out of the cabinets and stuffed them in her jacket pockets, to give to her girlfriend to strap down her breasts, so she could pass as a man on the streets of Brooklyn.

I see her young bones inside her walking down my block. When I look at her, I see her my way—mended like pottery inside and a liar still, which I don't mind. That's how she was taught love. By a thief in the night hospital.

She's still a bone eater. She smacks her lips at me on the block knowing forty years later that I know about the inside of her body and why she sucks.

Migdalia Garcia. That's her name.
Don't forget it.

What do you think happened?

Five

Would you like to see my body?

I'm sixty-four and I'm lucky:
I have both my breasts still,
safe, inside my suit.

My upper arms are big, 'cause my dad said life is hard, so he made us lift our weight every day before we went to school. My wing on the right side is lower than the one on the left; you will notice that right away. It kinda droops. I have been told that my clavicles are the sexiest part of my body. There's a photo of them recorded on a cell phone somewhere.

I can't lie down to be examined; it makes me feel like I will die. It scares me to expose the front of my chest without my arms covering it. I am feeling foolish in your room—like in the ladies room—a bull in a china shop.

Can you smell the years of sun on my skin making it rough like an elephant's hide, or are you too busy thinking that I look like Marilyn Monroe? When faced with only two choices, it's no surprise that you make the wrong one. I have two keys on my key ring and I get the wrong key every time. That's why I don't gamble.

The reason I get mistaken for a man is my neck. It's my Adam's apple that's throwing you off. My Adam's apple combined with my suit and tie is what's confusing you. My thyroid cartilage and my cricoid cartilage combine to challenge you.

I have been thirteen bodies in my life.
This is only one of them.

I cracked my pelvis. I broke my heels. I smashed my knuckles on my right hand. I smashed my knees in the woods. I fell off the porch and got a stick in my eye. The wind was knocked out of me when I smashed into a tree. I cut open my hand when my grandma died. I was on crutches for six months when I jumped off a fence. I had fourteen spinal taps curled up in a ball like a fetus. I was born with broken clavicles. I broke both heels. I got pneumococcal meningitis when I slept with a woman for the first time. I died for three minutes. I was in a coma for two weeks. I had mononucleosis and couldn't kiss a boy for a year. I had cancer on my face and got twenty eight stitches. I had a lump removed from my breast. I have lumps on my forearms and the front of my thighs where I store my original thoughts. I smashed out my two front teeth on the ice fighting over a girl. I had a baby.

August 15, 1969. New York City.

I had tickets to Woodstock but never made it out of town. When I went into labor they placed my feet up, head back. The nurse said,

"Lay down and I'll shave your pubic hair and give you an enema."

I told her I'd rather be in the mud and the rain listening to Jimi Hendrix.

My hips were growing wider and wider, like a doublewide trailer. Room enough for a whole family. My hips were keeping the door from shutting. When the doctor came in, he said there wasn't enough room for both of us.

I was a giant among men.

They pinned me to the table
like Gulliver,
thousands of ropes keeping me still,
shooting little arrows into me.

I told the doctor to think of my body as magic.

"Just relax," he said, smoking his pipe.

My daughter was ready to touch down on the planet, but she had to climb up and out of my womb, 'cause they had me tipping backwards, my feet in cold stirrups. (That was thirty-eight years ago before they discovered the law of gravity applied to women.) I was wearing a cosmic suit, with stars and moons and planets. They forced me to disrobe.

"I will kill you and your whole family if you don't get me out of this pain."

Six

I found a goldfish in my five-star hotel room in Seattle named Ashley. It was there to keep me company. In the morning I went to the desk and said I thought Ashley was lonely. They said it wasn't really Ashley anymore, because every morning the maids take all the goldfish to the basement and they swim together in a big tank. I said, "Can I see the tank?" and they said "No." They said goldfish have a memory of only twelve seconds, so she wouldn't remember her name anyway.

I don't believe anything they tell me about goldfish, or elephants, or penguins. I believe elephants have a long memory, but I don't believe goldfish have a short memory. Or that penguins miss each other.

Stacy's brother used to eat his aunt's goldfish out of the bowl when he was two. He liked how they wiggled down his throat making a fluttering feeling in his heart. He says that's why he became a doctor.

What do you think happened?

Who turned on the light in my throat and exposed all this? Didn't you hear me, inside, trapped and flapping?

Too late now, my bones are bleached by the dark cupboard. I'm gonna fold up my wings next to my side and give up the ghost.

And leave my bones to you.

Seven

Rattlin' Bones Song

I'm going to dig you up
Trace my hands along your bones
I want them near me
I leave traces of touch on your skin
So you're never, never, never alone
I want them near me, them rattlin' bones

My spleen, my appendix, my tonsils
Anything I don't need you can try
I want them near me
I'm going to dig up your bones
So that I can suck them dry
I want them near me, them rattlin' bones

Sweet bones that stick out and show me
where you bend
Lonely, angry, freaky bones
My hunger never ends
Two thousand years old teenage bones
Dug out of Egyptian sand
Two hundred and eight bones is all you need
To make an Elephant Man

The most painful thing about you
Is you can weep, but you can't smile
I want them near me
If I was quiet like you I'd be dead
But I could still love you if you gave me
enough time
I want them near me, them rattlin' bones

I touch you to make myself last
It's true my form is something odd
I want them near me
I maintain your remains with great respect
To blame me is to blame God
I want them near me, them rattlin' bones

I want them near me
Them rattlin' bones

(You're gonna turn over in your grave when you hear this song, baby.
I'm gonna dig twenty-feet down and I'm gonna find your coffin and I'm
gonna run my fingers along your bones. I'm gonna put a phone in there
so you can call me sometime. It's Friday night, your place or mine?)

Them rattlin' bones.

Eight

Sshh.

I hear voices in the background. Very low. I think they're talking
about my body. They're looking at my insides, on a machine.
They will never guess that I am a rogue by the shadow of my
insides. I have to keep my mouth shut, keep quiet, keep all my
holes closed, chew without opening my mouth and swallow
silently.

Deep inside me I have doors and locks and combinations, which I
keep well oiled and flexible. That's expensive. Inside me is
expensive.

This is the room next to a doorway on the third floor. There's a
tall window looking out into the sky with a difficult combination.
1958. It's night. All is dark and all are asleep, we can walk around
and listen to the sounds of people sleeping; their breath, their

pain is lit up in the dark like those fluorescent constellations you stick on the ceiling.

This is a cot in a hallway next to the window, where I sleep. A camp cot with pamphlets under my pillow—pamphlets explaining about silent things like ovulation and sin. Around the curved corner you can see me washing my grandmother's hair in the sink and slicking back my hair in the mirror when no one is looking. The bathroom door is locked. My mother has locked herself in there. I look through the crack. She is smiling and washing her hands over and over again. I will have to remove the hinges to get her out.

There is a knock at the front door. I see someone's back disappearing around the corner. I can hear ambulances approaching from the outside. This house has rooms that expand.

I open another door. This is the room my mother has warned me about. Writhing, half-eaten, half-skeleton corpses, having sex and eating too much, in agony from biblical words like gluttony and fornication and coveting your neighbor's wife.

I run outside, wouldn't you?

My mother is throwing dishes at the wall. They are shaking her back and forth, trying to knock some sense into her, yelling her name. It is her fault. She will need eleven shock treatments to get her to wash the dishes.

I tear at her like a hungry man, taking her body in my jaw and whipping her from side to side. My teeth sink in enough to get her attention, not to hurt her. Like a dog with a doll in its mouth, I fling her away and I jump onto the roof, but the house has a bad roof and slate shingles fall down making me slip off . . .

As I am falling I count the shingles . . .
I come from a family of counters.
I am counting now,
filling my brain with meaningless numbers:
I count the stairs
I count the panes of glass in the French door
I count by threes—
3, 6, 9, 12, 15
I count the audience
I measure countries and number organs
I colonize and categorize
I count the hours since you left,
but the numbers never add up.
I have to admit
they never add up.

Nine

The minute I laid eyes on you I knew you weren't going to make
my life any easier.

"You forget who you're talking to," you said as you leaned on the
doorframe.

It was as if the words were coming from the wrong part of your
body, from your middle instead of your chest and they felt like
you were right and I was wrong. I knew exactly who I was talking
to. Your eyebrows were cocked like your shoulders; you were
perched on your hips above your long legs.

"Aren't you lonely sometimes?" you said. I was wondering exactly
what you meant.

Did you really care if I was lonely? 'Cause of course I was,
sometimes, everyone is. You must mean something else. Women

like you say things, but mean something else a lot. It wasn't out of concern for me that you said it.

Maybe you were lonely.

You made a sound from the dangerous part of your body. Like an Italian sports car. You changed your center of gravity. You walked over to me and revved your legs just a little.

You took my hand and placed it between your thighs, so I could see what you were going through. I felt my cheeks get a crimson streak across them. My eyes sparkled like someone lifted the shades and turned on the lights. Finally, I was seeing something I could love. Something worth spending my precious time on. And you knew it.

> Pour me into a bag of fluids,
> you can have a piece of me.
> I'll be your pathological specimen.
> You can label, measure,
> strip and count me.
> You can squeeze me into a chest of drawers,
> bottle me in a jar.

> You can knock me down,
> step on my face,
> slander my name all over the place,
> you can do anything you wanna do,
> but uh uh honey. . .

Ten

A couple of hundred million years ago, before you were born, my body was joined together to form one land mass. Slowly my twelve plates started moving away from each other. My continents were dancing to the music of deep time. A dance of incredible slowness. Powerful enough to throw up the mountains and pour away the oceans.

My tectonic plates have always rubbed and exploded next to each other. Their edges are sites of intense geologic activity. The doctors gave me beta-blockers so I wouldn't 'cause a volcano, or an earthquake.

My tectonic plates float on a fluid-like asthenosphere, allowing them to undergo motion in different directions at the same time. Push-pull. Like having a girlfriend and a job and a family.

Sshh. You can hear the plates of my skull moving as I talk and the plates in my hips moving as I walk. Can you hear all my bones fitting together as I keep living?

I am sizematic. My back is slowly moving away from my hip-bone toward America, my vertebrae curving toward the horizon, slipping underneath the sea of love, taking a million years to crawl up out of the water.

I once had a gill removed from my neck. I've heard there are 22 bones in my skull, a globe balancing on top of my atlas. The bones are seamed together by tiny interlocking crocodile teeth. Seven bones orbit my eyes. A plough divides my right and left nostrils. A conch shell spins dust away from my lungs.

The reason the elephant man couldn't smile is because his zygomatic muscles were distorted. They are the muscles in the face that draw the mouth upward into a smile or a laugh. He's right here in this hospital. Talk to the right person and you can see the bones, the elephant bones, lonely and dusty and no one looking at them, no one paying to see them, no one touching and running their fingers gently along their surface.

When elephants are in must, tears flow freely from their eyes. I'm crying for you.

Tears are generated behind and within my upper eyelid, which is thicker and longer than my lower lid. Stuff is leaking out, draining from my eyes, dripping from my holes everywhere, tipping my head over like a tea pot, emptying my brain, pouring all the residue out onto the floor in a pile. There are little microbes swimming around and bits of bones and ancient ships and ancient germs and broken glass and pipes and coral and brick and dust of the ages and some giant teeth, a thigh bone and two old porcelain sinks washed up from an old slave ship, or a gay party boat, or a China tea schooner.

I'm crying for you. The flood keeps coming; it sweeps me off my feet. It's a flash flood. It's tearing up the hood like a glacier, ripping a new path through the rocks, sweeping away lifetimes. Sweeping everything away to the bedrock. It's raining too hard. It makes it impossible for me to walk and the water makes it impossible to breathe. I have to grab hold of familiar things: my mother; the magnolia tree in front of my grandfather's house, before they cut it down; my turquoise Plymouth; weeds at the side of my house. I am grabbing the whole time. It's not attractive, ladies and gentlemen.

> The water won't stop.
> The fields are becoming lakes the
> lakes of the moon,
> the lake of dreams, the lake of death.

> Come with me, my love,
> to the sea, the sea of love, the sea of waves,
> the sea of tranquility, the sea of rains,
> the bay of rainbows, the marsh of decay,
> the sea of nectar, the ocean of storms,

the sea of cold, the marsh of diseases,
the sea of fertility, the frozen pool,
the sea of crises.

The lakes on the moon don't even have any water in them, but I
have to reach up out of this place to find a little romance
somewhere.

Doctor, ain't there nothing I can take,
I say, Doctor, to relieve this belly ache?

Eleven

I am leaving these bones to science.

These big bones that get misidentified.

I wish I'da gave birth like an elephant, walking around. The little
weird body starts dangling down towards the ground. She starts
kicking it gently with her back legs, encouraging it to drop,
letting gravity do its job.

It doesn't matter, 'cause the sun is higher than when I started and
warmer and the shadows are not as long. There are only two
things in life right now that I am sure of—I will never die young
and, when something is real, it leaves a trace.

When they tested my blood in the hospital, they said it glowed at
night in the room and it was full of beautiful tiny objects floating
in an alphabet soup of pieces of bottle caps and Tupperware and
zip lock bags and thermoses and coffee cups and Mac books.

Everyone came to see its beauty. They held it up to the light of
the x-ray machine and they could see the shadows of a lifetime.

Forsythia bloomed three times this year. I can hear the unfamiliar sound of yellow in the winter woods and the quiet when the yellow freezes. The sound of time changes as I get older. I can hear the relaxing sound of my head clearing and my skin softening. If I was really quiet, I'd be dead. Leaving my body behind in the silence. I don't remember hearing that sound before. Looks like an Aurora Borealis, far away. It looks loud, like the night.

The underside of my fingertips holds all the memory of you. They are my delicate most sensible part. You will recognize them because I have white moons on them from high blood pressure. Endless information at my fingertips.

It's okay to die and leave your bones here with me.

I live in my breasts in a tent and sleep outside and cook and talk to the night animals that gather with me around the fire. Catching their eye, I look deep into wildness. If you look deep into *my* eyes, you will see the bushes moving just slightly, like a balmy smell in early spring, or the scary smell of burning hair that makes your nostrils flare.

I thought that's what thoughts look like when they are finished. Dusty and in a pile.

Now I know that molecules of dust are the future that exists by the side of the road that gets stirred up as I walk by.

> Like the small details
> that turned into the night,
> moving reflections on the ceiling,
>
> the turning of the tides in my flooded dreams,
> the giant step we didn't take,

the shocking speed of waxing and waning.

How, when you leave,
the earth quakes and the sun sets.

Eight Questions for Peggy Shaw

What is one of the most unexpected influences on your art?
Being dirt poor, being working class, having nothing to lose.

What's your most vivid memory from childhood?
Thinking I was born in the wrong body.

Who is your favorite villain of fiction?
God.

What was your worst job?
Go-go dancer at the Intermission Lounge in the red-light district in Boston.

What is your most marked characteristic?
My neck, and that Sean Penn looks like me.

What is your favorite euphemism?
Gender.

If you could ask one question to every person on Earth, what would it be?
Where do you find joy?

From the 8-Ball interview series, Walker Art Center, Minneapolis, June 2005.

What question do you wish we asked you?
Is a million dollars too much to pay you to come and perform? Plus
a per diem.

Selected Bibliography

PRIMARY SOURCES:
INTERVIEWS, CORRESPONDENCE, REVIEWS,
AND FEATURE STORIES

Interviews and Correspondence

Dolan, Jill, and Peggy Shaw. Personal e-mail correspondence, 2 Apr. 2009.

Dolan, Jill, and Peggy Shaw. Personal e-mail correspondence, 3 Apr. 2009.

Dolan, Jill, and Jaclyn Pryor. Interview with Peggy Shaw, Austin, TX, 19 Apr. 2005.

Dolan, Jill, and Jaclyn Pryor. Interview with Lois Weaver, Austin, TX, 23 Apr. 2005.

Dolan, Jill, and Jaclyn Pryor. Interview with Sue-Ellen Case, Austin, TX, 15 Apr. 2005.

You're Just Like My Father

Desimone, Lewis. Rev. of *You're Just Like My Father*. *San Francisco Sentinel* 23 Aug. 1995.

Holden, Stephen. Rev. of *You're Just Like My Father*. *New York Times* 26 May 1994: C19.

Hurwitt, Robert. "Peggy Shaw Scores a 50-Minute KO." Rev. of *You're Just Like My Father*. *San Francisco Examiner* 21 Aug. 1995.

Lipsky, Jon. Rev. of *You're Just Like My Father*. *Boston Globe* 23 Sept. 1995: 23.

Minkowitz, Donna. "Daddy Is a Dyke." *Village Voice* 28 June 1994: 31–32.

Phillips, Julie. "Theatre." Rev. of *You're Just Like My Father*. *Village Voice* 7 June 1994.

Shewey, Don. Rev. of *O Solo Homo*. *Advocate* 1 Sept. 1998: 55–56.

Soyer, Julia, and Caitlin Dean. Rev. of *You're Just Like My Father*. *Gay Community News* 21.2 (fall 1995).

Stuart, Jan. Rev. of *You're Just Like My Father*. *New York Newsday* 31 May 1994.

Topiary, Samuel. "Thriving by Surviving: Butch Theatre Queen Peggy Shaw." *San Francisco Bay Times* 10 Aug. 1995.

Yang, Jacob Smith. "Shaw's Parent Trap." Rev. of *You're Just Like My Father*. *South End News* 28 Sept. 1995.

Menopausal Gentleman

Beeler, Heidi. "Rebel with a Cause: Peggy Shaw's *Menopausal Gentleman*." *Bay Area Reporter* 22 Jan. 1998.

DeLombard, Jeannine. Interview with Peggy Shaw. *Philadelphia City Paper* 10–17 Apr. 1997. http://citypaper.net/articles/041097/article001.html. 25 Mar. 2004.

Donahue, Anne Marie. "Warm Flashes: *Menopausal Gentleman*." *Boston Phoenix* 27 Mar.–2 Apr. 1998.

Fanger, Iris. "Actor Puts 'Men' into Menopause." Rev. of *Menopausal Gentleman*. *Boston Herald* 25 Mar. 1998: 43.

Ferguson, Marcia. "Menopausal Gentleman." Rev. of *Menopausal Gentleman*. *Theatre Journal* 50 (1998): 374–75.

Fuchs, Derek J. "When It Comes to Growing Older, She's a Perfect 'Gentleman.'" *Ticket* 17 Jan. 2003: 11.

Green, Westry. "Hot Flashes and Mustaches: Performance Artist/Actor Peggy Shaw Goes through the Change." *HX for Her* 5 June 1998: 12.

Groover, D. L. "Chatting with the 'Menopausal Gentleman.'" *Houston Voice* 14 May 1999: 26.

Halliburton, Rachel. "On the Fringe: *Menopausal Gentleman* Drill Hall." *Independent* [London] 154 (Apr. 1999): 11.

Hammond, John. Rev. of *Menopausal Gentleman*. *In Theater* 26 June 1998: 13–14.

Hill, Logan. "Lady and Gentleman . . ." Rev. of *Menopausal Gentleman*. *New York* 18 Dec. 2000: 219.

Hogan, Jane. Rev. of *Menopausal Gentleman*. *Back Stage: The Performing Arts Weekly* 38.50 (1997): 48.

Huntington, Richard. "Stories and Solidarity." *Buffalo News* 30 Oct. 1998: G35.

Huwig, Pam. "A Menopausal Gentleman." *Curve* 9.1 (1999): 6.

Jones, Arnold Wayne. "Your Average Butch Grandma: Cross-Dressing Lesbian Performance Artist Peggy Shaw Stages *Menopausal Gentleman*." *Dallas Voice* 10 May 2002.

King, Loren. "Panting Nights: Peggy Shaw's Sad and Funny Show about 'Change of Life' Entrances at the BCA." *Bay Windows* 26 Mar.–1 Apr. 1998.

Lucas, Craig. "Peggy Shaw." *Bomb* 69 (1999): 34–39.

Palmer, Caroline. "Gentlemen Prefer Menopause." Rev. of *Menopausal Gentleman*. *Culturata* 23 June 1999. http://www.citipages.com/databank/20/968/ article7689.asp. Accessed 22 Mar. 2004.

Rawson, Christopher. "Peggy Shaw's *Menopausal Gentleman* Cuts Across Gender Lines." *Pittsburgh Post-Gazette* 20 Jan. 2003: D6.

Rosenstein, Anna. "Challenging Preconceptions with Charm." *Pittsburgh Post-Gazette* 18 Jan. 2003: B6.

Rosenstein, Brad. "Ebb and Flow: Tides of Performance, *Menopausal* to *Amorphous.*" *San Francisco Bay Guardian* 14 Jan. 1998.

Russell, Mary. "Sharp-Dressed Woman to Talk about the Menopause." *Irish Times* 15 Apr. 1999: 15.

Russo, Francine. "Flash and Burn." Rev. of *Menopausal Gentleman. Village Voice* 16 June 1998: 172.

Siegel, Ed. "Peggy Shaw Bends the Gender Fences." *Boston Globe* 25 Mar. 1998: C6.

Sime, Tom. "Nature Has the Last Laugh: Shaw's 'Menopausal Gentleman' Tackles Body vs. Identity." *Dallas Morning News* 16 May 2002.

Steel, Mel. "All Change: She's Out, She's Butch, and She's Passing as a Man." *Guardian* [London] 6 Apr. 1999: 6.

Walter, Kate. "Hot Flashes: Peggy Shaw Weathers Menopause." *New York Blade News* 14 Nov. 1997: 28.

Williams, Patrick. "Different Seasons: Peggy Shaw Hit Middle Age and Became a Menopausal Gentleman." *Dallas Observer* 9 May 2002.

Yang, Jacob Smith. "Peggy Shaw Revs Up Performance-Art Genre." *South End News* 11 Sept. 1997.

To My Chagrin

Alvin, Rebecca M. "Shaw Delivers a Mesmerizing Tour de Force." Rev. of *To My Chagrin. The Cape Codder* 9 July 2004.

Cragin, Sally. "Peggy Shaw Explains Her Chagrin." Rev. of *To My Chagrin. Boston Phoenix* 25 June–1 July 2004. http://www.bostonphoenix.com/boston/events/theater/documents/03929633.asp. Accessed 8 February 2011.

Harrison, Sue. "Shaw Is a High-Performance Engine with Smooth Moves." Rev. of *To My Chagrin. Provincetown Banner* 8 July 2004.

Jefferson, Margo. "An Easy Segue from Tender to Tough." Rev. of *To My Chagrin. New York Times* 13 Oct. 2003.

Martin, Deborah. "'Chagrin' takes on Heavy Topics without the Weight." *San Antonio Express-News* 23 Oct. 2001.

Mathis, Sommer. "Queer Performance Found Start in Drag." Interview with Peggy Shaw. *Daily Bruin* 6 Feb. 2003: 87.

Melo, Frederick. "Of Hot Rods and Cold Truths." Rev. of *To My Chagrin. Cape Cod Times Online* 5 July 2004.

McNulty, Charles. "Rock-a-Bye Granny: Shaw Air-Guitars an Unbiased Lullaby." Rev. of *To My Chagrin. Village Voice* 14–21 Oct. 2003.

Morgan, Susan. "What's Driving Miss Peggy." *Anchorage Daily News* 6 Feb. 2004: E1.

Perille, Gina. "Butch's Eye View." Rev. of *To My Chagrin. Bay Windows* 14 July 2004. http://www.baywindows.com/news/2004/07/14/Fun/Butchs.Eye.View-693435.html. Accessed 25 Sep. 2004.

Perille, Gina. "There's Much to Shaw's *Chagrin.*" *Boston Globe* 7 July 2004: F5.

Reynosa-Davis, Heather. "Lesbian Grandmother Magnetic in Out North *To My Chagrin.*" *Anchorage Daily News* 10 Feb. 2004: D2.

Thomas, John W. "Passing on Her Butchness." Rev. of *To My Chagrin*. *LIP* 1 July 2004. http://www.what.org/peggylip.htm. Accessed 25 Sep. 2004.

Shaw on Shaw

Shaw, Peggy. "Gosh Dirt." *Telling Moments: Autobiographical Lesbian Short Stories*. Ed. Lynda Hall. Madison: U of Wisconsin P, 2003. 235–42.

Shaw, Peggy. "How I Learned Theatre." *Cast Out: Queer Lives in Theatre*. Ed. Robin Bernstein. Ann Arbor: U of Michigan P, 2006. 25–29.

Shaw, Peggy. *You're Just Like My Father. O Solo Homo: The New Queer Performance*. Ed. Holly Hughes and David Román. New York: Grove, 1998. 175–98.

SECONDARY SOURCES:
ESSAYS ON GENDER, SEXUALITY,
FEMALE MASCULINITY, PERFORMANCE

Allison, Dorothy. *Skin: Talking about Sex, Class, and Literature*. Ithaca, NY: Firebrand Books, 1994.

Bergman, S. Bear. *Butch is a Noun*. San Francisco: Suspect Thoughts Press, 2006.

Blau, Herbert. *Blooded Thought: Occasions of Theatre*. New York: Performing Arts Journal, 1982.

Bornstein, Kate. *Gender Outlaw: On Men, Women, and the Rest of Us*. New York: Routledge, 1994.

Bornstein, Kate, and S. Bear Bergman, eds. *Gender Outlaws: The Next Generation*. Berkeley, CA: Seal Press, 2010.

Bruckner, D. J. R. "A Jazz Artist and Father Turns Out to Be a Woman: 'The Slow Drag,' American Place Theatre." *New York Times* 18 Apr. 1996. http://theater2.nytimes.com/mem/theater/review.html?html_title=&t ols_title=SLOW%20DRAG,%20THE%20(PLAY)&update=19960418&b yline=By%20D.J.R.%20BRUCKNER&id=1077011432796. Accessed 9 Apr. 2009.

Burana, Lily. "Conversation with a Gentleman Butch." *Dagger: On Butch Women*. Ed. Lily Burana, Roxxie, and Linnea Due. San Francisco: Cleis Press, 1994. 114–19.

Butler, Judith. *Gender Trouble*. New York: Routledge, 1990.

Butler, Judith. "Performative Acts and Gender Constitution." *Performing Feminisms*. Ed. Sue-Ellen Case. Baltimore: Johns Hopkins UP, 1990. 270–82.

Cameron, Loren. *Body Alchemy: Transsexual Portraits*. Pittsburgh: Cleis Press, 1996.

Canning, Charlotte. *Feminist Theatres in the USA: Staging Women's Experience.* London: Routledge, 1996.

Case, Sue-Ellen. *Feminist and Queer Performance: Critical Strategies.* London: Palgrave Macmillan, 2009.

Case, Sue-Ellen. "Making Butch: An Historical Memoir of the 1970s." *Butch/Femme: Inside Lesbian Gender.* Ed. Sally R. Munt. London and Washington, DC: Cassell, 1998. 37–46.

Case, Sue-Ellen. "Playing in the Lesbian Workshop: Migrant Performance Labor." Lecture. Performance as Public Practice Program, Department of Theatre and Dance, University of Texas at Austin, 15 Apr. 2005.

Case, Sue-Ellen. "Tracking the Vampire." *differences* 3.2 (summer 1991): 1–20.

Case, Sue-Ellen. "Toward a Butch-Femme Aesthetic." *The Lesbian and Gay Studies Reader.* Ed. Henry Abelove, Michele Aina Barale, and David M. Halperin. New York: Routledge, 1993. 294–306.

Case, Sue-Ellen, ed. *Split Britches: Lesbian Practice/Feminist Performance.* New York: Routledge, 1996.

Copper, Barbara. *Ageism in the Lesbian Community.* Freedom, CA: Crossing Press, 1987.

Crawley, Sara L. "Are Butch and Fem Working-Class and Antifeminist?" *Gender & Society* 15.2 (2001): 175–96.

Cvetkovich, Ann. *An Archive of Feelings.* Durham: Duke UP, 2003.

Davy, Kate. *Lady Dicks and Lesbian Brothers: Staging the Unimaginable at the Wow Café Theatre.* Ann Arbor: U of Michigan P, 2010.

Davy, Kate. "Outing Whiteness: A Feminist/Lesbian Project." *Theatre Journal* 47 (1995): 189–205.

Delany, Samuel. *Times Square Red, Times Square Blue.* New York: New York UP, 1999.

Diamond, Elin. *Unmaking Mimesis: Essays on Feminism and Theatre.* London and New York: Routledge, 1997.

Diamond, Elin. "We Keep Living." *Theatre Journal* 62.4 (December 2010): 521–27.

Dolan, Jill. "Performance, Utopia, and the 'Utopian Performative.'" *Theatre Journal* 53 (2001): 455–79.

Dolan, Jill. "Practicing Cultural Disruptions: Gay and Lesbian Representation and Sexuality." *Critical Theory and Performance.* Ed. Janelle Reinelt and Joseph Roach. 2nd ed. Ann Arbor: U of Michigan P, 2009. 334–54.

Dolan, Jill. *Presence and Desire: Essays on Gender, Sexuality, Performance.* Ann Arbor: U of Michigan P, 1993.

Dolan, Jill. *The Feminist Spectator as Critic.* Ann Arbor: U of Michigan P, 1991.

Dolan, Jill. *Theatre & Sexuality.* New York: Palgrave Macmillan, 2010.

Dolan, Jill. *Utopia in Performance: Finding Hope at the Theatre.* Ann Arbor: U of Michigan P, 2005.

Epstein, Rachel. "Butches with Babies: Reconfiguring Gender and Motherhood." *Femme/Butch: New Considerations of the Way We Want to Go.* Ed. Michelle Gibson and Deborah T. Meem. New York: Harrington Park Press, 2002. 41–57.

Feinberg, Leslie. *Stone Butch Blues: A Novel.* Ithaca, NY: Firebrand Books, 1993.

Frankenberg, Ruth. *White Women, Race Matters.* Minneapolis: U of Minnesota P, 1993.

Freistadt, Berta, and Marg Yeo. "A Cruel Trick: Menopause/Aging." *Out the Other Side: Contemporary Lesbian Writing.* Ed. Christian McEwen and Sue O'Sullivan. London: Virago Press, 1988. 30–39.

Garber, Marjorie. *Vested Interests: Cross-Dressing and Cultural Anxiety.* New York: Routledge, 1992.

Grosz, Elizabeth. *Volatile Bodies.* Bloomington and Indianapolis: Indiana UP, 1994.

Halberstam, Judith. *Female Masculinity.* Durham: Duke UP, 1998.

Halberstam, Judith. *In a Queer Time and Place: Transgender Bodies, Subcultural Lives.* New York: New York UP, 2005.

Hollibaugh, Amber. *My Dangerous Desires: A Queer Girl Dreaming Her Way Home.* Durham, NC: Duke UP, 2000.

Hollibaugh, Amber, and Cherríe Moraga. "What We're Rollin' Around in Bed With: Sexual Silences in Feminism: A Conversation Toward Ending Them." *The Persistent Desire.* Ed. Joan Nestle. Boston: Alyson, 1992. 243–53.

Ji Hye. "Performing Female Masculinities at the Intersections of Gender, Class, Race, Ethnicity, and Sexuality." Diss., University of Texas at Austin, 2007.

Kadi, Joanna. *Thinking Class.* Boston: South End Press, 1996.

Keating, Ann Louise. "Interrogating 'Whiteness,' (De)Constructing 'Race.'" *College English* 57.8 (1995): 901–18.

Kelly, Jennifer. *Zest for Life: Lesbians' Experiences of Menopause.* Melbourne: Spinifex Press, 2005.

Kennedy, Elizabeth Lapovsky, and Madeline C. Davis. *Boots of Leather, Slippers of Gold: The History of a Lesbian Community.* New York: Routledge, 1993.

Loulan, Joann. "Butch Mothers, Femme Bull Dykes: Dismantling Our Own Stereotypes." *Dyke Life.* Ed. Karla Jay. New York: Basic Books, 1995. 247–56.

Loulan, Joann. "Now When I Was Your Age: One Perspective on How Lesbian Culture Has Influenced Our Sexuality." *Lesbians at Midlife: The Creative Transition.* Ed. Barbara Sang, Joyce Warshow, and Adrienne J. Smith. San Francisco: Spinster Book Company, 1991. 10–18.

Lynch, Lee, and Akia Woods, eds. *Off the Rag: Lesbian Writings on Menopause.* Norwich: New Victoria, 1996.

Mahoney, Martha R. "The Social Construction of Whiteness." *Critical*

White Studies: Looking Behind the Mirror. Ed. Richard Delgado and Jean Stefancic. Philadelphia: Temple UP, 1997. 330–33.

Newton, Esther. *Margaret Mead Made Me Gay: Personal Essays, Public Ideas.* Durham, NC: Duke UP, 2000.

Newton, Esther. *Mother Camp: Female Impersonators in America.* Chicago: U of Chicago P, 1979.

Newton, Esther. "My Butch Career: A Memoir." *Queer Ideas.* Ed. Center for Lesbian and Gay Studies. New York: Feminist Press at CUNY, 2003. 83–97.

Russ, Joanna. *The Female Man.* Boston: Beacon Press, 1986; 1975.

Salamon, Gayle. *Assuming a Body: Transgender and Rhetorics of Materiality.* New York: Columbia UP, 2010.

Salamon, Gayle. "Boys of the Lex: Transgenderism and the Rhetorics of Materiality." *GLQ* 12.4 (2006): 575–97.

Sandell, Jillian. "Telling Stories of 'Queer White Trash.'" *White Trash: Race and Class in America.* Ed. Matt Wray and Annalee Newitz. London and New York: Routledge, 1997. 211–30.

Solomon, Alisa. "Theater: The Wings of Desire: WOW Café Celebrates 20 Years." *Village Voice* 9 Jan. 2003: 61.

Solomon, Alisa. *Re-dressing the Canon.* New York: Routledge, 1997.

Torr, Diane, and Stephen Bottoms. *Sex, Drag, and Male Roles: Investigating Gender as Performance.* Ann Arbor: U of Michigan P, 2010.

Valerio, Max Wolf. *The Testosterone Files: My Hormonal and Social Transformation from Female to Male.* Berkeley: Seal Press, 2006.

Wildman, Stephanie M., with Adrienne D. Davis. "Making Systems of Privilege Visible." In *Critical White Studies: Looking behind the Mirror.* Ed. Richard Delgado and Jean Stefancic. Philadelphia: Temple UP, 1997. 314–19.

Wittig, Monique. "The Point of View: Universal or Particular?" *The Straight Mind and Other Essays.* Boston: Beacon Press, 1992. 59–67.

Acknowledgments

There is no such thing as solo. And it is difficult trying to figure out how to acknowledge the love and support of the many for the one. The following is a flawed attempt to say thank you to those who have seen this project I call my life through its many phases.

My friends, family, and supporters for life . . . Lois Weaver, Shara Antoni, Ian Antoni, Stacy Makishi, Vick Ryder, Suzy Willson, Matthew Boals, Jill Lewis, Karena Rahall, Amy Meadow, Judy Rosen, Judith Katz, Telma Abascal, Joy Tomchin, Kristine Altweis, Laura Shaw, and Cooper Square Committee.

Past and present partners and inspirations . . . Split Britches, Deb Margolin, Stormy Brandenberger, Vivian Stoll, Susan Young, Paul Clark and the Clod Ensemble, Stafford (the true Menopausal Gentleman), Rebecca Taichman, and James Neale Kennerley.

The people and places that opened doors . . . in New York, Ellie Covan, Mark Russell, WOW Café, LaMama, Dixon Place, PS 122, the Hemispheric Institute for the Study of Politics and Performance; in San Antonio, Steve Bailey, Esperanza Center for Peace and Justice, and Jump Start; in London, Clod Ensemble's Performing Medicine, Queen Mary University; and Hampshire College.

Those who looked after many, many details . . . Judy Boals, Tracy Gentles, Anneliese Graham, Rose Sharp, Lori E Seid, Cynthia Baker, and all the technicians and designers who make things possible.

Those who argued, critiqued, and documented what they saw . . . Jill Dolan, Elin Diamond, Sue-Ellen Case, and Alisa Solomon.

Those who went before and have gone on . . . Norma Shaw, Jimmy Shaw, Liz Hammerstrom, and Ellen Stewart.

And for this book . . . Jill Dolan, Lois Weaver, Jaclyn Pryor, and LeAnn Fields at the University of Michigan Press.

Printed and bound by CPI Group (UK) Ltd, Croydon, CR0 4YY

13/04/2025

14656533-0005